The Ghost Town Collectives

&

other stories for the Anthropocene

BRITTNEY CORRIGAN

Books may be purchased in quantity and/or special sales by contacting the publisher. All inquiries related to such matters should be addressed to:

Middle Creek Publishing & Audio
9161 Pueblo Mountain Park Road
Beulah, CO 81023
editor@middlecreekpublishing.com
(719) 369-9050

First Paperback Edition, 2024
ISBN: 978-1-957483-25-2
Cover Art: Collage, DALL-E Inspired background with digital design elements added, creating a hybrid artwork, David A. Martin
Cover Design: David A. Martin
Internal Images: Royalty Free Clipart
Endplate Image: Dodo bird (Didus ineptus) - vintage engraved illustration - "Dictionnaire encyclopédique universel illustré" By Jules Trousset - 1891 Paris

The Ghost Town Collectives

&

other stories for the
Anthropocene

BRITTNEY CORRIGAN

Middle Creek Publishing & Audio
Beulah, CO   USA

Contents

for the endlings, with apologies

Woolly

For the past three months, I've been in charge of the petri dishes in which we're growing mammoth hair. Jasmine is in charge of the blood cells, and Pete from Omaha handles the fat. I labored head down like a work horse to get into this particular grad school—even though I'm not an East Coast, Ivy League kind of person—just so I could be in this lab with Dr. Chapelle and his team. What I'm learning here is important, beyond resurrecting the woolly mammoth. It's about reversing extinction. Staring death in the face and backing it down. I'm here to help save my sister.

She and I are identical twins, and our parents thought it would be delightful to give their daughters palindromic names: Hannah and Elle. To go with our last name, which is Renner. We make it a game to ask people to guess what's in the middle. We became the Palindrome Twins from day one. Hannah and I are the mirror image of each other. I'm right-handed, but Hannah is a southpaw. The whorls of our hair and fingerprints curl in opposite directions. Standing eye to eye with my sister is like looking at my reflection in the stillness of a lake.

I've always been the scientist. First dinosaurs, then chemistry sets, and then I convinced my parents to pay for taxidermy lessons. A disgruntled-looking squirrel is still perched on my bookshelf back home in Oregon, posed mid-forage with an acorn in his witchy paws. Eventually, I moved on to microscopes. Hannah willingly donated specimens—hair from her brush, blood from her finger that we pricked with a pin from our mother's sewing kit—and I'd magnify them under the lenses next to samples of my own, trying to see if I could tell us apart.

Hannah is the athlete. At least she was until the diagnosis a couple of years ago. She was training to be an Olympic swimmer, in college on a full scholarship. But then the cancer came, taking her down with the stealth of a sleeper shark. It snuck up on her, vicious and strong, and has been tearing at her little by little ever since. She's moved back home with my parents while the doctors throw everything they have at her body. But nothing sticks for long. Now she's preparing for a bone marrow transplant next month—my healthy, matching stem cells flowing into her bloodstream—hoping it might stop the cancer from circling back. Until then, I'm here in this lab, with its promise of something miraculous. Something that could annihilate her cancer from the inside out.

It sounds like science fiction, but de-extinction is a very real thing. And not just to prove that we can do it—be the species to reincarnate beasts that lived on Earth long before we did or to try to fix our mistakes, like the passenger pigeon or the black rhino. No, bringing back large grazing animals to the tundra might help save the permafrost. The animals that used to stamp around snuffling for grass in the snow helped the cold penetrate the ground to keep it frozen. But they're all gone now, and the long-insulated layers are starting to warm and melt, releasing huge amounts of greenhouse gases into the atmosphere.

When Hannah and I were kids, our parents would take us hiking in the Cascades, up past the timberline to where everything opens up. Expansive meadows of wildflowers and the sky going on forever. Even in the summer, the air was crisp and cool, the wind tangling our opposite-curling hair as we scanned the rocks for quick movements of pika and marmots. Despite the chill, we'd shuck our sweatshirts, run into the fields of flowers, and spin ourselves dizzy until we collapsed in the grass. We'd pretend we were alpine animals, unbothered by the altitude or temperature, living our lives amid the snowy peaks. Those memories are tainted with sadness now, like a heavy beast pressing its feet down on my chest. The chemo means Hannah's always cold these days, right down to her bones.

Jasmine and Pete from Omaha help keep my spirits up. Jasmine draws me little pictures on our lab notes—whimsical critters with thought bubbles drifting above their foreheads, somehow knowing just what to say. Jasmine is quiet and slight, her dark hair artistically arranged in bundles atop her head—a new configuration each day. If she were an animal on the tundra, she'd be an arctic hare, everything about her cautious and hushed. Jasmine holds her pipettes carefully, as if they were creatures whose trust she's trying to gain. Beside her slender wrists, the ruby dishes of blood cells look beautiful and bright.

I have trouble sleeping, sometimes drag myself into the lab like I've walked across a vast distance to get here. *Have some coffee*, Pete from Omaha will say cheerily, handing me a steaming cup. Everyone calls him Pete from Omaha, never just Pete, because that's what he calls himself. *Hi, I'm Pete from Omaha, nice to meet you.* Under his lab coat, Pete from Omaha sports wildly colorful shirts with bold patterns. He exudes energy and humor, even though he's very serious about the work. Pete from Omaha would stand out on the tundra like a tropical bird, clearly in the wrong climate altogether.

I'm not sure what kind of animal Hannah is now. She used to be some kind of seal, fast and happy in the water. She could lap the pool fast as any sea creature, over and over. At her high school meets, buzzed on the smell of chlorine and the blurry echo of pool noise, I'd watch her dive and vanish into the water, swimming away from me. I'd hold my breath with her, waiting for her to surface and make her first stroke. She'd spin and flip turn at the end of the pool, doubling back to me again. Now I'm starting to think of her in the same way I do the woolly mammoth. Something that used to be. Something I'm trying to bring back.

Before I left, I'd sit with Hannah during treatments, and we'd do the research together, looking for the most promising new developments in the field. Her cancer is acute myeloid leukemia. It mutates her blood cells—dividing and dividing and dividing until her blood forgets how to be her own, how to be like mine. When we came across a news story about the Chapelle Lab, it seemed like a magical thing, right out of one of our childhood storybooks. A place where a sorceress might conjure a creature from nothing but bones and a few strands of hair.

Even though it meant me leaving her while she's sick, Hannah insisted that I come out here to study, assured me she'd be fine until I got back. Whenever I had doubts about going, she'd put her arm around my waist and lean my head into her shoulder. As if she were propping me up instead of the other way around. *You've got to do this, Elle,* she told me. *I know this is going to help people like me.*

Hannah's always been determined like that, so sure and confident that it seems she can make anything happen. She manifested a win for every swimming race. Even though her body's struggling right now, I have to believe she'll beat the cancer, too. Otherwise, how could I be here on the other side of the country monitoring stem cells, waiting for them to sprout hair?

What we're doing in the lab is editing genes. It turns out the Asian elephant is 99.96% woolly mammoth, which sounds like a lot, but it's a difference of about 1.4 million mutations. We're finding the differences and then putting mammoth DNA into elephant cells, trying to get them to change. Mammoth blood, hair, and fat could help elephants cope with cold temperatures. I love picturing woolly Asian elephants roaming around Siberia, where scientists are working to recreate the Pleistocene mammoth steppe, hoping to protect the permafrost and all the rest of us along with it. We're creating a chimera to defend against the damage we've done.

But I'm really here to learn the technique: Clustered Regularly Interspaced Short Palindromic Repeats. A family of DNA sequences found in the genomes of bacteria that help them fight viruses and which has taught us how to modify the DNA of other cells. The same technique that tricks elephant cells into developing like mammoth cells could one day teach immune cells to attack cancer cells in humans. When Hannah and I first heard about CRISPR, with its surprise of repeated DNA sequences—just like our names—we knew it was what I was meant to do. A palindromic cure for one of the Palindrome Twins.

Every morning, Jasmine and Pete from Omaha and I are in the lab, checking on the cells. Now that it's late autumn, the mornings are dark and chilly, and the peacefulness is like a salve. Campus still tucked in and sleeping, not even the birds awake yet. Sometimes there's an overnight frost, and the ground crunches a little as I walk to the lab, that marvelous squeaky sound that's part crumpling tissue paper and part branches rubbing window glass. My breath forming little ghosts. Mornings like that, I imagine I'm a caribou making my way across the Arctic steppe. I can almost feel the antlers sprouting from my skull, their weight bending my weary head toward the ground.

When I text Hannah now, she'll only write to me in palindromes. We used to do this as kids. We'd spend hours after school coming up with elaborate palindromic communications, a code to keep secrets from our parents. We devised every possible sequence of words, became experts at deciphering each other's messages. I don't know if she's gone back to our cryptic language to let me know we're still connected through the thousands of miles, or because she's in so much pain, or so tired, she can only manage a handful of words. *Elle. Drawn onward, Elle*, she writes, to let me know she's still fighting. *In words drown I*, meaning, it's too hard to talk right now. *Live evil.* Yeah. As if I didn't know that's what this is.

When I'm tending to the cells in the lab, I think about how Hannah's blood is like my blood. Her hair is like my hair. All those years staring through microscopes, small offerings of our girl bodies laid out end to end on slide after slide. We are more similar than elephants and mammoths. We are 100%. Twin caribou navigating the ice. But then a polar bear comes, and it only mauls one of us. Why did it choose her instead of me?

Borrow or rob? Hannah asks when I text her. How much time does she have left? *Not a tub, but a ton.* The bath is not the same. She misses swimming. *Doom mood.* This is a chemo week. *I prefer pi*, I message her. The digits of pi go on infinitely. I would do anything, anything. Hang on. I'll decipher the puzzle. I'm working as fast as I can.

And I am. I stay late at the lab every evening, peering through the microscope as if I could watch the cells morph from elephant to mammoth right before me. I pore over textbooks and journal articles until my eyes are too sore to take in more. Somewhere in all of this data is the answer to why Hannah's body is sick. What I can learn to make her better. The recipe for turning her immune cells into that mythical chimera, coursing through her veins and hunting down the leukemic blasts. Goring the purple bodies until they shrivel, until no cancer remains.

The week of Thanksgiving, Jasmine and Pete from Omaha and I figure out a plan for the cells. My labmates both have places to go. Families with circumstances. Same as me, except I can't afford to go home. Hannah's treatments are expensive—intense chemo to prepare her body for the transplant—and we're saving everything for when I come home in December for the procedure. When I left for grad school at the end of the summer, Hannah and I knew I wouldn't be back until winter break, wouldn't be able to be with her after treatments or comfort her when she lost the last of her hair. But I can feel her here with me, willing me to win this race. Her blood is my blood. And part of my heart beats all the way across the country to her. *Boom, boom, boom.* I send it out over all the landscapes in between.

When I think about donating my marrow, I imagine what it would feel like to be swimming inside her veins, restoring her blood to match mine. I imagine the delirium of waking up from the anesthesia, Hannah's hand on my arm, feeling like we are one again—sisters, twins. Before we divided. Before we were mirror images, right-handed and left-handed and making our opposite ways in the world.

In the lab, Jasmine shows me her routine with the blood cells, her hair assembled with metal knitting needles choreographed in perfect angles around a messy bun. I force myself not to nod off as I watch her hands move hypnotically around the petri dishes, meticulously preparing microscope slides. Pete from Omaha has typed out instructions for the fat cells. A flourish of fonts and bullet points on fluorescent pink paper is taped to the lab's refrigerator door. Thanksgiving morning, it will just be me, quietly tending to the cultures. Just me and the fibroblasts as I try to remind myself what I have to be thankful for.

I call Hannah on Thanksgiving Eve, to tell her for the millionth time how sorry I am to not be there. She sounds broken down, too weak to talk. She wants to text instead. *Bird rib*, she writes. I'm not sure if she means the turkey or how delicate her body feels. So I just write, *Decaf and DNA faced*. I'm taking care of myself. I'm doing the work for her. *Do geese see God?* she asks. This doesn't sound like Hannah and her usual optimism. I'm not sure how to respond. I want to believe that for every animal, there is something to come home to. The ghosts of the mammoths lumber around me, making me shake in my chair. Please, I think, let's not talk about the after. Let's talk about the more.

Thanksgiving morning, before sunrise, the deserted campus is so quiet I think maybe I really am in Siberia, nothing but stillness as far as I can see through the chilly fog. I've hardly slept, and through my bleary eyes the shifting predawn shadows are arctic foxes. They pop their heads up out of the snow and then sprint away, vanishing completely, even when I squint after them to see where they've gone. The campus buildings rise out of the mist, behemoth-like, and I fold myself between them, navigating my way by routine familiarity alone.

Emerging from the darkness as I approach it each morning, the science building always seems to have dozens of eyes—row upon row of yellow-lit, modern windows stacked up into a giant's staircase, a pathway from lawn to sky. Once I'm inside, the deserted hallway comes at me with a fluorescent hum that feels almost alive. The vacancy is tangible—itself a presence in the absence of my labmates. I pull the heavy doors closed behind me, listen as the building reverberates with the sound of the lock scraping back into place. It's soothing rather than frightening. Like I'm inside the belly of something sure and strong.

As I make my way toward our lab, I can hear movement behind the door, a sound like something shifting weight. I figure Dr. Chapelle has come in to check on something. I call out his name, my voice echoing through the building like a sonar ping. I open the door a crack. The light is off, and even the shadows are so thick as to be invisible. There's a shuffling. An unmistakable animal huff.

There are plenty of animals in the building, but none that would be near our lab. Mostly rats and mice—nothing large, or dangerous. But I can tell that whatever's in there has a heft to it. And an odor that reminds me simultaneously of a stable and freshly fallen snow. Though it feels utterly deserted, there must be other people somewhere in the building, tending to animals and projects just like I'm tending to the cells. I try to listen more carefully, the way Hannah and I used to do as kids, whispering late into the night, then hurriedly quieting as our parents headed for our bedroom door. I strain to hear beyond the lab. *Hello?*

Another huff and a deep lowing sound come out of the darkness. Then the sharp, clean smell of chlorine tendrils past. Like someone installed a swimming pool overnight. I'd know that smell anywhere—the smell of Hannah's swim meets—and the memories smack me in a sudden wave, make me feel like I'm starting to drown. But I steady myself, reach in and feel for the light switch. Click it on. Then open the door slightly wider so I can see in. Standing wedged between the refrigerator and the emergency wash station is a woolly mammoth, eight feet tall with thick, tawny hair and tusks twisting precariously over the counters of beakers and flasks. Pete from Omaha's bright pink instructions are a rumpled casualty on the floor.

The mammoth and I blink at each other. My heart is beating triple time, so I know I'm not dreaming. I'm going over all the sci-fi movies Hannah and I have watched together, instantly cross-referencing them with every class I've taken, every textbook I've read. But it all ceases to matter rather rapidly, as I watch the mammoth's tusks list closer to where the samples are housed. I have to get it out before it destroys the lab.

Mammoth? I whisper, my voice shaky and small beside the creature's woolly bulk. But it seems gentle, and scared. I hold out my hand like I would to a dog, venture a couple of steps closer. Inexplicably, it still smells like chlorine, and stable and snow, but also like my childhood bedroom. The wooden bunkbeds Hannah and I shared. Summer sneakers and strawberry lip gloss and library books. Something about that smell makes me brave. I curl one hand around the tip of a tusk. The mammoth lowers its head, leans into my hand, as if it knows I'm trying to help. *Okay, mammoth,* I say. *Here we go.*

I back up slowly, maneuvering the curvature of its tusks around the delicate instruments of the lab. It's a wonder that it hasn't broken anything yet. How long had it been waiting here? Did it step out of a petri dish fully formed? The mammoth follows me willingly, placing one fuzzy foot in front of the other so quietly it seems to be floating. Its trunk sways gently, and it sighs softly, completely at ease. Its eyes are huge and intent, as if it has something to say. Those eyes are exactly the same color as my own.

Though it seems we won't fit, we wedge safely through the lab door, like our bodies are made of clouds or sand, and we pause in the hallway. Dr. Chapelle isn't here, there are no other scientists, and clearly no one else in the labs. The building is eerily silent, except for the nearly animate fluorescent hum. I'm still holding on to the mammoth's tusk as I formulate a plan. The university is at the edge of the city's big public park, and it's only about a mile through the greenbelt to the zoo. There must be someone there feeding the animals. Maybe they'll know what to do with a creature 99.96% elephant.

In a daze, I start walking, steer the mammoth out through the building's big double entry doors. We don't see a soul. The world is impossibly peaceful and uninhabited, like the hush of a snowy morning, but there's no snow. There's just the crunch of my shoes against the frosted grass, the mammoth's animal breathing. When we get to the park's little manmade lake, barely starting to ice over, the mammoth stops short, won't move another step. *Mammoth?* I coax. *It's okay. It's only a little farther.* But the mammoth just looks out over the lake. Then it swings its trunk to the side and wraps it around my waist. Just the way Hannah does with her arm when we're together, a gesture that always makes me feel like we are one being standing in the enormity of the world. My head on her shoulder. Two halves of one whole.

My breath catches, and I stand perfectly still. The mammoth is warm, and comforting, like it knows something about me. Like my sadness is palpable. It leans its bulk into me just a little, the coarse tendrils of its coat against my cheek, the jumbled smell of chlorine and lip gloss and beast overwhelming. Then it uncoils its trunk, pulls its tusk out of my hand, and starts to run toward the lake. I reach out to stop it, but the mammoth is remarkably fast, and strong. Determined. All I'm left with is a handful of wiry hair.

It's then I feel the cleaving. Like I'm being split in two. The mammoth is swimming now, out to the center of the lake through the floating ice, smooth and easy as if it's done this all its life. Its trunk is raised above the water, and it turns back to me for a moment, almost waving, and closes its eyes, those perfect reflections of my own. I feel as if I'm breaking open. I buckle to my knees on the frost-brittle grass, both hands over my heart, trying to keep it from falling out of my chest. And then the mammoth disappears, breaking up like fogged breath over the surface of the lake.

And I know it. My sister is gone. I think of all those petri dishes in the lab, waiting for me to come and take care of them. How there's still work to be done, though I'm struggling to remember what it's for. I think of Jasmine and Pete from Omaha, probably just waking up among their families, beginning the holiday preparations in their kitchens. I'm dizzy, and the cold from the ground is starting to work its way up through me. I wish like anything that I were home.

My phone sounds an unearthly alarm in the quiet of the sun coming up over the lake. But I let it ring and ring, knowing it's my parents, dreading the news. It wasn't supposed to happen this quickly. We were sure she had more time. *Mammoth!* I call out, sending my voice out like a bugling elk, listening to it dissipate through the frost-handed trees. *Hannah!* Then, just a whisper, *You buoy.* A little life raft of a palindrome. It's all I can manage, trying to hold on to the other half of myself, looking for a way to stay afloat.

I open my fist, but the last of the mammoth's hairs are already starting to disintegrate in my palm. I stare hard at them, trying to magnify them back into being. But then the wind picks up, and I watch as the withering hairs curl and lift from my hand. I try to reclasp them, but I'm too late. I feel it in my blood, my bones, right through to my marrow. I'm too late. I can't see my reflection in the lake, can't see anything through my overflowing eyes. What remains of the little hairs drifts across the water like a wisp of smoke, vanishing as it moves away from me. Nothing doubles back in return.

The Great Unconformity

Mica sits on the front porch of the cabin, looking out at the unwelcoming expanse of the Oregon Outback. She wishes she were anywhere but here, in a house that is not her own with a father who is not her father. She's supposed to be texting her friends and having sleepovers. She's supposed to be spending the summer before high school walking around her neighborhood with a gaggle of teens, a slushie in one hand and someone else's sweet, nervous fingers in the other. Instead, she's trapped here in the unrelenting heat with no internet and no phone service and no other people besides her rockhound mother and her newly-minted stepfather, who she refuses to like even though he's ridiculously likeable.

They'll only be here for a month, but to Mica it feels like a distant horizon of days that seems to recede even as she walks toward it, tipping over the edge of the dusty alkaline Earth. Mica had wanted to spend the whole summer at home, despite the fact that her mother had whittled the evidence of her father's existence down to two plastic bins that she stashed in a corner of the basement before Gale, the father-who-is-not-Mica's-father, moved in. Mica had managed to snag one treasured item that jutted from the "throw away" pile like the peak of an iceberg: the journal from her father's last trip three years ago, the one during which he disappeared. She keeps it with her at all times, a battle her mother has let her win.

Mica's parents were both studying geology when they met, two college students with rocks and minerals knocking about in their heads. Her father used to say that her mother was like a geode: rough and volcanic on the outside but hiding something beautiful and shimmering within. Mica knows this to be true. Petra is the kind of woman who has walked through fire and hardened herself against it.

Both of Mica's parents have the same degree, though they took their training in very different directions. Petra is a professor at the university, her academic brain rooted squarely in geologic truth, and she spends her days preparing young students to take on problems of energy resources, natural disasters, and climate change. Still, her crystalline heart loves a good treasure hunt: obsidian, agate, the thrill of an unearthed gem. When Mica was little, she had loved rockhounding, too. Now she can barely remember the rush of holding a bit of jasper or amethyst in her palm.

Her father, on the other hand, had never been content with studying what the Earth offered up to him. Craig was more interested in what *wasn't* there: layers of the planet's surface that should have been present, but were missing. The irony of this is not lost on Mica, who sits on the shady back porch of the little cabin with her father's journal open on her lap, trying to hide from the heat that's already building in the high desert morning. The journal had been discovered in a small backpack containing maps and supplies found at the site in Arizona where her father had vanished. And no one—not forensic experts nor skilled trackers—had found anything else. Not a footprint, not a drop of blood, not a single strand of hair.

The journal is open to a page imprinted on Mica's brain. Across the spread of weathered paper is a drawing her father rendered meticulously with colored pencils: layer upon layer of rockface stacked along the wall of a great crevasse. Subtle hues of brown and red press against a line that's darkened across the length of the drawing. Words hem the page in her father's neat, angular script. Words Mica has read again and again: *Cambrian explosion, Proterozoic, Tapeats sandstone, Vishnu schist, uplift, Snowball Earth.* And across the top of the page, in large capital letters: *The Great Unconformity.*

"That again?"

Her mother's voice, pitched somewhere between sympathy and irritation, comes from over Mica's shoulder. Mica stiffens as she closes the journal in her lap and swivels her head. Petra is gathering up her long, silver-flecked hair and winding it into a messy bun on top of her skull. She closes her eyes and tilts her head from side to side as she threads the thick strands into place. Mica's own hair is sheared into a pixie cut, and as the sweat beads at the back of her neck, she's thankful that she decided to chop it short on the first day of summer vacation.

"So what?" As her mother slides a clip into the perfectly imperfect bun, Mica tips the journal toward her heart.

"I was hoping while we're here you might spend a little less time with that thing and a little more time with Gale."

Mica turns her head away and lets out a microscopic sigh. *That thing* is her one connection to her father, the puzzle of what happened to him that she is determined to solve. She has grown tired of her mother's uncanny ability to move toward the future when the only thing that Mica wants is buried in the past.

"You can't make me let him go." Mica crosses her arms over the journal and stares out at the endless landscape of sagebrush and cracked earth. The cabin is perched at the edge of an immense, dry lakebed: prehistoric and inhospitable.

"Come on." Her mother's voice softens as a harrier hawk whirls overhead, dives into the needlegrass at the lakebed's rim. Mica thinks of the fat little ground squirrels that forage around the cabin, imagines one of them startled by the grip of the hawk. Petra brushes her fingers over Mica's shoulders. "We're going to Rabbit Basin today, to look for sunstones."

Once Petra walks back into the cabin, Mica opens the journal again, gently traces the dark line across the penciled tiers of rock. *Where did you go?* She closes the book slowly, reluctant to leave its carefully penciled world, and follows her mother inside.

*****

Rabbit Basin is 90 minutes from their cabin, and Mica is grateful for the air-conditioned car. Petra loves to drive, especially in wide-open places, and Gale appears content to go along for the ride. His build is slight and folds easily into the passenger seat, and his thick, salt-and-pepper hair is wild on top of his head, even though the windows are rolled up. As her mother and Gale chirp back and forth in the front seats, Mica trains her ears on the hum of the engine and tunes out. She's brought a notebook and pen and is scribbling out a letter to her father.

Mica has been writing to him ever since he disappeared. Letter after letter, detailing not only the minutiae of her days, but also what she's managed to learn from hours of internet searches about the area where he was last seen. She pictures him walking through the narrow slot of the remote canyon, making notes, running his hands along the rock walls towering around him: ridges stacked like pancakes, layered like pastry.

Between the 1.7-billion-year-old strata and the 545-million-year-old sedimentary rock, there is... nothing. The Great Unconformity: over one billion years of missing geologic time for which her father spent his career trying to find an explanation. Mica has read articles on tectonic plates, speculation about biblical floods, and accounts of travelers who have heard mysterious drumbeats and whispers of ghosts. In her letters to her father, she recounts scientific studies, fringe theories, folklore. She addresses the envelopes to *Craig Wesley, The Great Unconformity, Blacktail Canyon, AZ*. So they can't come back to her, she never includes her return address. She doesn't know where the letters go.

"You alive back there?"

She looks up to see her mother's hazel eyes lifted toward her in the rearview mirror.

Mica rests her hands on top of the letter. "Yup."

"We're almost there." Her mother's eyes settle back on the road.

Though they've been driving for miles, the landscape is all the same: flat and brown and dotted with pale, gray-green sagebrush. Rugged outlines of mountains in the distance.

"What are you writing about?" Gale twists his body to face her. Irritation rises in Mica, even though he's being kind, seems genuinely interested. But she isn't going to tell him about the letters. Her mother doesn't even know about them. Mica buys the stamps with her allowance, mails the letters at the post office three blocks from their house.

"Deer."

That's true, even if it's only a partial truth. Blacktail Canyon is named for the mule deer that inhabit the plateau to its north. In her letters, Mica often responds to the stories her father used to invent for her at bedtime: imaginary tales inspired by his travels. In this story, he is lying in a field at dusk, surrounded by sleeping deer. The light from the setting sun filters through their immense ears, turning them a rosy pink. He counts racks of antlers, black-tipped tails. When the heat-miraged ball of the sun slips behind the rim, the dreams of the deer rise from their velvety hides like mayflies, populate the sky with stars. *How did you know those were their dreams?*

Mica wrote. She imagines her father telling her, *Because they were filled with mountain lions and fire.*

"I made a piece about deer once," Gale offers.

Though she hasn't lifted her head from her notebook, Mica can tell Gale is still looking at her, waiting for her to respond. Begrudgingly, she turns her attention to him. Despite herself, she admires her stepfather's work. Gale is a photographer, with an Ansel-Adams-meets-Andy-Warhol sensibility. He photographs landscapes and then superimposes images of people and objects in repetitive rows, eerie commentaries about the human impact on the planet. Mica can't help but be drawn into his pieces, taken with how they splice what's real with what's not.

Mica gives in to her curiosity, allows the image of her father to slip momentarily aside.

"What kind of piece?"

Gale's face brightens, and Mica feels the irritation creep back in.

"Images of taxidermy deer heads layered over a photo of the woods," Gale continues. Then he turns back around in his seat before Mica can respond. "Oh, we're here!"

Here looks exactly like all the land they've just driven through, save for the addition of a tiny shade structure, a few picnic tables, and a handful of RVs. When Mica steps out of the car, the heat envelops her body, and she feels an immediate thirst that seems to come from beneath her skin. A cluster of clouds is on the horizon, heading their way, which she hopes will cause a temperature drop when they roll in. Mica takes a long drink from her water bottle, puts on the stupid sun hat Petra insisted that she bring, and holds out her hands for the sieve and geology pick that Gale passes to her from the stash of tools in the hatch of the car. She tucks them into her backpack next to her notebook and her dad's journal.

"Just stay within the orange markers," Petra says as she leads the way into the rocky dust. "This is the public collection area."

As Mica walks, the ground seems to come alive. Flecks of sunstone glitter everywhere in the soil, throwing light back at the sky. Mica thinks of her friends, imagines the sun sparkling on the surface of the pool where they are probably all hanging out together right now, without her. Her boots feel heavy and hot, and resentment builds in her body, sweltering and fierce.

They hike past a few other heat-braving rockhounds until they are all alone; although, true to the basin's name, several jackrabbits dart around them, in and out of clusters of greasewood and sage.

"Perfect!" Petra drops to her knees in the dirt, as if this particular spot is somehow distinct from everything around it. Mica sighs and squats next to her mother. Gale wanders off with his camera and tripod, though Mica can't imagine what there is to photograph in this place at this overexposed hour of the day.

Mica takes the pair of gloves Petra hands to her and unzips the pick from her pack. She hasn't gone rockhounding with her mother in a long time, not since before her dad disappeared. But the rhythm of it comes back to her as she chips and sorts through the soil beneath her hands, falling into sync with her mother's seasoned forearms. As they dig, memories of trips she and her parents took sift to the surface of her brain. Flashes of hiking together down trails and along riversides, their pockets full of rocks.

"Aha!"

Within a few minutes, Petra has unearthed a small, intact sunstone. She smiles, her hazel eyes partially shaded beneath the flop of her hat brim, and playfully nudges Mica's elbow, the way she used to do when Mica was younger. "Do you know what makes a sunstone a sunstone?"

Mica shakes her head, knowing her mother is going to shift into professor mode, and wipes her sweaty brow with the back of her hand. Petra turns the stone in her palm and dusts it off, then rubs it until its surface gleams. The berry-sized stone shimmers in her mother's hand, alternating shades of butterscotch and amber. "It's feldspar crystal, formed in lava. Most of them are light yellow, like this one."

Her mother holds the translucent stone up to the blue backdrop of sky and admires it from every angle. "Some are green or red, due to higher concentrations of copper. This is the only place in the world where you can find this variety of sunstone. Cuprian Labradorite. It's Oregon's state gem."

Petra hands the stone to her daughter. Mica has to admit to herself, it's a beautiful thing. It seems to glow from within, like someone has lit a small fire at its center. Mica thinks of her father, lost somewhere in a vast cathedral of rock. His heart a buried beacon, waiting to catch the light. It feels to Mica like something is melting between her ribs, softening the strata she's built up around her heart. The sadness lodges in her throat, and she can't muster any sort of response to her mother. Mica hands the stone back, turns her eyes to the ground.

The bank of clouds shadows them moments later, and the two of them search for another hour in the welcome respite from the heat. Mica finds several sunstones, one with just a hint of green, like a tiny animal inside is winking at her. Her mother ends up with a grapefruit-sized sack full of the stones, one of which is just the faintest shade of red, a hard-won prize extracted from a pile of partially-decomposed rock. When Gale joins them again, mother and daughter are dusty and hungry. As Gale hands Mica a peanut butter sandwich from his pack, she is actually grateful to see him.

On the trek back to the car, the occasional lizard crisscrosses their path, looking for just the right place to cool down. The sun wins out over the clouds, ripening their faces in the desert heat. Mica is relieved once again to tuck into the back of the car and aim the air vent directly at her face. They are all quiet on the drive to the cabin, leaning into the curves of the road.

That evening, Mica finishes the letter to her dad. *We found sunstones today*, she writes. *They are the color of honey. They are the color of deer.* She pictures her father running his fingers along the unexplained juncture of two entirely different planetary lifetimes: one formed of dark gray, crystalline granite and one of sandstone, rich with fossils, evidence of life. *They are the color of sandstone. They felt warm in my hands. I was almost happy.*

With no post office for miles, Mica instead turns over the paper and addresses the back of the page. She steps out onto the porch of the cabin. A fierce wind has descended on the desert, silhouettes of dust devils pushing across the dry lakebed. Mica offers the letter to the desert night, watches it disappear into the gusting dark.

*****

Two weeks into their stay, Petra announces she's going to drive to the nearest town, about 30 miles away, for fresh produce and a full tank of gas for their next excursions. Mica jumps at the chance to go with her. There might be service enough to text her friends, and she thinks that perhaps she can actually mail her most recent letter to her dad. Gale stays behind, to capture the dramatic sky around their cabin. Thunderclouds have been gathering all morning, darkening and breaking the summer light.

Mica's most recent letter is full of snow and ice. She knows about Snowball Earth, has investigated all of the words and phrases from her father's last sketch over the past three years. She knows it's one likely theory to explain the Great Unconformity: planet-wide roaming glaciers eroded a third of Earth's crust and dumped the sediment into the slushy oceans, where it was gobbled up by the mantle's tectonic plates. Mica likes to imagine the planet one billion years ago, completely covered in ice. Like one of her mother's brilliant gemstones.

In the letter, Mica has invented a story about her father and Snowball Earth. He is riding a glacier like a dragon across the land, the icy monster feasting on boulders, devouring whole mountains as it courses toward the sea. Her father is clad in ice, his hair a sharp tangle of icicles. As the glacier dragon plunges into the ocean, her father dives toward the Earth's core, swerving through the subduction zone as plates collide all around him. Then he surfaces, bobbing like a seal. He swims for the shore, stands at the rim of a canyon and shakes off the ice so it clatters and bursts around his feet. *Weren't you cold?* Mica writes. *Weren't you afraid?* She imagines his answer. *It was so cold, I almost forgot who I was. But then I remembered you.*

When they arrive in town, Petra gasses up while Mica checks for phone service. She has one bar. For a moment, she has two. She tries to send a few texts to her friends, but they all bounce back. She finally gives up. As they park in front of the little general store, Mica spots the post office across the street. "I'll meet you in a minute," she tells her mom. "I want to mail a postcard to a friend."

"Alright, be quick," Petra says. "I want to get back before the rain starts. Looks like this is going to be a big one."

Mica heads across the street as her mother disappears into the store. The sky is definitely foreboding: deep gray clouds throwing their shadows ahead of them as they approach, the wind picking up.

The post office is tiny, just one room with an older woman camped out behind the counter. She smiles as Mica walks up.

"What d'ya need today, young stranger?" The woman is friendly, probably knows everyone in town.

"Hi," says Mica. "Um, I just need one stamp." She sets her letter on the counter as she searches her pockets for the dollar bill she knows she stashed somewhere.

"You're going to need a zip code." The woman eyes the letter, then looks up at Mica with one eyebrow raised. "And a return address."

Mica is suddenly embarrassed. What was she thinking, mailing one of her letters to nowhere from this little town in the middle of nowhere?

"Uh, yeah, ok, um, I think I remember the zip code," she says, pulling a pen from her pack. Mica feels a strange sort of panic as she writes her name and home address in the corner of the envelope, then hesitates as she tries to invent a string of five numbers.

"Here, I can look it up for you," says the woman, and she places her hand on the letter. Mica tries to pull it back, but it's too late.

"Wait a minute." The woman is staring at the envelope like she's seen a ghost. "This is crazy, kiddo, but I think I have something for you."

"What? I don't even live here."

"Welp, the world is a funny place." The woman sets down Mica's letter and turns to rifle through a bin at the end of the counter marked "UNDELIVERABLE". She produces a small envelope, thin and frail-looking, and waves it toward Mica. "Just came in yesterday. This you?"

Mica feels her heart stop. Sharp and hard, a raw ruby in her chest. There's her name, *Mica Wesley*, on the front of the envelope. Her name, printed in neat, angular script. Her name, next to a tiny pencil drawing of a deer. The return address, just: *Blacktail Canyon, AZ.*

"Oh," she manages to say, hardly a whisper. "Yes, that's me."

The woman places the envelope in Mica's hand. It's soft and light, delicate as fresh snow.

Mica closes her eyes a moment, wills her heart to start again, and then grabs the letter she brought in off the counter. "Thank you," she says quickly. "I've got to go!"

"You don't need a stamp anymore?" the woman calls after her.

Mica pushes open the door. She stands frozen outside the tiny post office, an envelope in each hand. A low growl of thunder tumbles toward her like a slide of scree.

Mica pockets the letter she wrote, sits down on the sidewalk right where she is. The street is deserted, everyone likely sheltering from the coming storm. Holding the little envelope with both hands, she stares at her name again, her father's handwriting so familiar, so close. Then she slides a finger beneath the flap and opens the envelope slowly, carefully.

Inside, there is nothing but dust.

*****

"Mica!"

Her eyes snap up, away from the envelope now vibrating in the building wind. Petra is calling to her from across the street.

"Mica, come on! What are you doing? We have to go!"

Her mother is hurriedly stowing groceries in the car, her long hair whipping about her face. Big drops of rain begin to fall, multiplying by the second. Mica presses the envelope to her chest and runs for the car. By the time she slides into the passenger seat, she's half-soaked.

"Whew!" Petra throws the car into reverse, then pulls out into the pouring rain. "What were you doing back there?"

Mica's not sure how to start. *I've been writing letters to Dad and he wrote me back. I think.* She looks down at the envelope, still pressed against her chest. She doesn't say anything.

"Mica?" Her mother glances over quickly, but then turns her eyes back to the road, navigates through the thick sheet of rain. "Mica, what is that? What do you have?"

"It was at the post office," she manages, choosing her words carefully, the ruby in her chest now embering with heat. "For me."

"Well, that's odd," Petra says. "Did one of your friends figure out how to write to you?"

"Not exactly." The whole landscape has gone dark. The clouds are black, black, black, and the wind is pelting the car with rivers of water.

"Well, what is it then?" Petra has slowed the car, is staring straight ahead with her hands tight on the wheel.

"It's from Dad." The words leave her mouth, but Mica doesn't remember deciding to say them.

"What? Ugh, I can't drive through this. We're going to have to pull over and wait it out." Petra eases the car to the side of the road, leaves it idling. The wipers are slashing back and forth at top speed. Mica isn't sure her mom even heard what she said.

Petra looks over at Mica, hands still on the wheel. "Who did you say it was from?"

Mica flashes to a memory of herself as a child, sitting between her parents in a zipped-up tent that quivered with wind, echoed with the *splat-splat* of mountain rain. She was six years old, and they had gone camping deep in the wilderness, on a fossil hunt. Mica had woken up in the night, afraid of the storm. She remembers her mother stroking her hair, her father singing to calm her. She remembers holding a smooth piece of petrified wood in her hand.

She was scared then, and she was safe, and she was scared. Mica feels like that now, her hands folded over the envelope.

She'll believe me. She'll see his handwriting, and she'll believe me.

Mica peels the envelope away from her damp chest and hands it to her mother. "From Dad," she says. "It's from Dad."

Petra stares at her. "What are you talking about? That doesn't make any sense." She takes the envelope from Mica, holds it up to the storm-ridden light. "What am I supposed to be looking at here?" she asks. "There isn't even anything inside."

Mica takes the envelope back, and she feels the breath go out of her. The envelope is so wet it's nearly disintegrating, and the words and drawing on the front have melted into a spidery smudge.

"Mom," she says. "You have to believe me. It was from Dad. It was his handwriting and everything." A flash of lightning scissors the sky above the sagebrush, momentarily brightening the inside of the car. Petra's face is pale, hardened.

"Cut it out, Mica," she whispers. Her face flushes, her eyes narrow and bore into Mica's own. "Your dad is *gone*. He's not. Coming. Back. He's *dead*."

Mica feels her mother's words in her bones. Neither of them have ever said it out loud. They've never had a funeral. *Dead.* Mica feels the tears brim in her eyes, spill down her cheeks. *It isn't true, it isn't true, it isn't true.* "Mom…" she starts, part word, part sob.

"No." Petra stares at her daughter, her hazel eyes fiery, lit by lightning, lit from within. "I've had enough of this, Mica. Mooning over his journal every day is bad enough. Now you're making things up? It's time to move on."

"Oh, like you?" Angry words pile up on Mica's tongue, and she can't stop them avalanching into the space between herself and her mother. "Moving on to the first guy who came along like Dad was never even there? Like you could just sweep his memory away?"

"It's not like that, Mica." Tears are gathering at the edges of Petra's eyes, her stiff shoulders starting to crumble.

"Dad's *alive*," Mica insists and passes the envelope toward Petra again, as if her father's words might somehow reappear.

But her mother's face hardens again. She looks away from Mica and pulls the car back onto the road. Guns it through the rain, right into the heart of the storm. Mica keeps her eyes pinned shut all the way back to the cabin, and neither of them says another word.

*****

For the better part of the next week, Mica doesn't speak to her mom or Gale. Her mother gives her a wide berth, but Gale tries to broker a peace, offering to make cookies, or watch one of the movies from the cabin's stack of DVDs. His attempts only make it worse, and it's maddening to Mica that he can't see how he is contributing to the rift. Eventually he leaves her be. He and Petra let her eat meals in her room and stay behind when they go out exploring. But not this morning. Her mother flings open the curtains and stands over Mica's bed.

"Get up," she says, but not unkindly. "It's thunderegg day, and you're coming with us."

It's as if the conversation in the car never happened. As if the envelope doesn't exist. And it barely does. Mica dried it out, pressed it into the back of her father's journal, but it's such a sorry-looking thing that she now doubts her earlier conviction. The magic of that lettering, of the little deer—now completely indiscernible—is slipping away, its own kind of missing time.

And Mica actually does want to look for thundereggs. She remembers learning about them from her mother when she was younger, but this trip to Oregon is the first time they've gone someplace where the rocks-that-aren't-really-rocks can be found. She dresses quickly, only half-shedding her anger but glad for one last diversion before she can go back home.

Thunder Egg Lake is an hour's drive from their cabin, and the digging pits are in a remote site a few miles beyond. They've come equipped for the long hike, and early enough to beat the heat. As they walk, Petra barrages Gale with facts about their quarry. He's listening attentively as she tells him how the thundereggs formed millions of years ago in the gas pockets left by rhyolite lava, the baseball-sized spheres with their colorful cores wildly different in appearance depending on their location. Mica imagines holding the rough treasure in her hand, cutting into it to see what kind of beauty hides inside.

Well into the hike, the three of them have spread out along the unpeopled trail. Gale is out ahead and has paused to train his camera lens on the sky, where a pair of golden eagles is circling. Petra has fallen far behind, stopping often to examine one rock or another. Mica walks impatiently between them, ready to get to their destination.

As she nears Gale, she hears it. A vibrating buzz, followed by the telltale, maraca-like sound. She stops short and looks behind her for her mother, who is out of sight. Mica scans the ground in front of her until she sees the snake, coiled in the center of the trail. The rattler is just a few feet from Gale, from the slender rise of his bare ankles. Doesn't he hear its warning? He backs slowly toward the snake, still looking through the camera lens, his face tilted toward the sky.

It all happens in a glacier of a moment. A tightness gathers in Mica's chest. She doesn't shout, can't make herself call out to Gale.

She can only watch as he takes one last step backwards. Right into the loop of the snake.

The rattler strikes Gale's calf, then unlatches its jaws and streaks away. Gale makes a burbled kind of shouting noise and drops to the ground, grabbing his leg. His camera clatters into the dirt beside him. Petra suddenly rushes past Mica, who wills herself to follow her mother. Already Gale's leg is swelling. Petra's face is crumpled with horror as she kneels beside him and runs her fingers over a flock of hives blooming around the bleeding wound.

"What happened?" Mica's mother looks up, pleading.

Mica can't speak, stands over the two of them, paralyzed.

"Mica!" Petra shouts. "Did you see what happened?"

Gale is now struggling to breathe, writhing on the ground. Mica's mouth is so dry she can hardly form her lips around the word. "Rattlesnake," she half-whispers, turning her face away. The ruby in her chest has shattered, shards cutting at her from within. One of the eagles cries out, and the pair banks and flies off.

Petra snaps into a sort of trance. "He's having an allergic reaction," she says. "We have to get him to a hospital."

They are at least two miles from their car, and the nearest hospital is 20 minutes from that point. Their phones have no service. Gale is growing weaker, and his eyelids droop as his face begins to swell. "Mica," says her mother, with exceptional calm. "You have to help me carry him."

They struggle Gale's arms around their shoulders, heft his lean body up between them. He tries to walk, but he is fading, his head collapsing onto his chest. Together, Mica and her mother stumble their way back down the trail. It seems to take forever, and they have to stop every few feet to let him rest. By the time they get Gale to the car, he is barely breathing. By the time they get him to the hospital, it is too late. The doctors administer the antidote, but his reaction to the venom has advanced too far. Less than two hours after being bitten, Mica's father-who-is-not-her-father is dead.

*****

The drive back home is long and silent. Mica doesn't know what to say to her mother, whose sad eyes never stray from the road ahead. Grief has made Petra ashen and weary, all her light gone out. Mica sits in the passenger seat and holds her green-eyed sunstone. She turns it over and over in one hand, tries to calm the roil of guilt and sadness and shame. She wants the comfort of her father's journal, but she knows better than to look at it in Petra's presence. She's afraid to pull out her notebook and write him a letter, either, so she settles herself by composing one in her mind, instead.

She pictures her father standing in Blacktail Canyon, barefoot in a little pool framed by a tunnel of golden rock. She imagines him placing his hand on the line of the Great Unconformity, at that meeting of two worlds that should never have met. *What does it feel like?* Mica asks him. *Is it very hot where you are? Very cold?* She pictures him among the fossils deep inside the sandstone. Resisting erosion. Holding his place in time.

When at last they pull into their driveway, it's late. The modest houses of their tidy street are quiet, all the neighbors in for the night. Just the faintest hint of mid-summer sunlight is fading into deep cobalt blue. The merest dusting of stars. As Petra shuts off the car, Mica sees that someone is standing on their doorstep, cast in shadow. She looks over at her mother, who is leaning her head against the steering wheel, unmoving. Mica opens the car door slowly, straining to see who is waiting.

She takes one tentative step toward the house as her eyes adjust to the near-dark. The figure's hair is glistening, impossibly, with tiny icicles. He is soaking wet, shoeless, caked with mud. In one hand, he holds a single antler, its points outlined in silhouette. The other hand clasps a sheaf of letters.

In Mica's chest, a thunderegg breaks open. The weight of a billion years lifts from her skin, streaks its colors toward the sky. Mica runs, closes the gap between herself and her father in no time at all. She reaches out for him, and his body stutters like a mirage.

I was lost somewhere, he says to her, his voice thin and soft as dust. *But then I remembered you.*

The Vault

Silje has walked the four kilometers from town, dragging an empty sled behind her. She has come for the seeds. Though they are not hers, isn't this why the seeds are here? They are here in case of devastation, or disaster, or war. In case of hunger. Silje stands before the wide steel doors of the vault, the entrance rising out of rock and snow. It's as if the mountain had opened its mouth and swallowed most of the structure, leaving only a rectangular hull jutting back toward the sea. The narrow face of the vault, above the entryway, is illuminated by a square of mosaiced prisms, mirrors, and steel. These carefully puzzled shards also extend along the roof, ending at its halfway point as the concrete wedge of the vault slopes down to meet the mountain. Silje loves when these quadrates glow turquoise and green against the northern lights. But that display, and the darkness, are still some weeks away. Now, it is autumn, on the cusp of winter, and the vault basks in rose-tinted light. Silje stands at the entrance doors, which are almost always sealed, and adjusts her wool hat firmly over her ears. She watches her breath condense into mist in the horizoned polar sun.

*****

Birna has been wandering the island for weeks. She can hardly remember her last true meal. She swam and swam through waters with no ice, no seals. Birna remembers reindeer from seasons past, but now there are no reindeer, either. She has been stalking the rising water, eating seaweed off the rubbled shore. She has raised her head to the midnight sun, waiting for the terns with their black caps, their bodies but a mouthful. But the terns have not come. She has looked for the mottled eggs of rock ptarmigans, and discovered none. Birna's hunger is like a thorned thing in her belly. A thorned emptiness that should be filled with the flesh of seals. When Birna eats a seal, she can sense the cold water, feels what it's like to rise and breathe through a hole in the ice. Her heavy, thick-furred body glistens, agile and slick. When she is muzzle-deep in blubber, instead of horizonless sea ice, she sees the snow caves, the ringed pups in their lairs. Now, Birna feels only her own body, weakening under the blue roof of sun.

*****

For many years, Silje received seeds from all over the world and deposited them in the vault. Packed in boxes, the seeds came on planes to the northernmost airport on Earth. Inside the boxes, the seeds were sealed in foil packets and glass vials. The boxes were unloaded from the planes and brought by van to where the road ends at the entrance to the vault. A few decades ago, when the vault was built into the side of the mountain, the ocean lapped 131 meters below. The waters of Isfjorden rise and rise each year—coming for the airport, for the town—but they will never reach the door of the vault, where Silje stands bundled against the cooling air. The vault's location was chosen because it is high, the landscape un-quaked, the rock and permafrost many meters thick. And now Silje has come for the seeds, though she knows she cannot plant them in the spoiled ground. Still, the seeds are the only promise of food that remains. And Silje is the only one left who can get into the vault.

*****

Once, Birna leapt onto the back of a narwhal when it surfaced between ice floes. Up came the spiraled tusk, and then the blotched, unbeaked head. Birna had been sitting completely still, waiting for the moment when some creature below would need to come up for air. Usually this was a seal—the ones with ring-dappled hides or the ones with bearded faces—but that day it was a narwhal that toothed its way through the polar ice. When the beast's breath sounded with a hollow, humid puff, Birna threw the full weight of her body upon the grey ridge of its back, locked her jaws around its blow hole, and tore. As the blood touched her tongue, she felt as if her teeth were growing longer, spindling and plunging deep into the whale's thick skin. When she hauled its large body up onto the ice, cleaved it into sinew, muscle, and bone, her black skin flushed with the easy intimacy of the pod, a memory of diving close together deep into the utter dark. Between Birna's paws, the narwhal's undone tusk clattered and scraped against the glacial ice.

*****

Silje pulls open the heavy steel door. Before her, a tunnel extends hundreds of meters into the mountain's core. The overhead lights are still working, powered by generators that Silje will not be able to refuel when they give out. Silje watches her breath hover and disappear, hover and disappear as she walks farther and farther into the vault. At the end of the tunnel is another set of steel doors, frosted over and secure. She gives a strong tug and pulls the cold doors open. Deep in the vault, the tunnels and storage rooms are carved into permafrost, ensuring the seeds stay perpetually frozen. In recent years, as crop after crop failed against hurricanes, floods, and blistering sun, many countries retrieved their seeds from the vault. Seeds that could withstand higher temperatures, or wetter soil. Silje watched carefully boxed and sorted and catalogued seeds leave the vault until the millions of varieties dwindled to thousands. With the island's power plant closed and the internet long unreachable, she no longer has access to the database that would tell her which seeds are left and detail what is in each box from Canada, Nigeria, Syria, Australia, Brazil. Silje produces a well-guarded key from her coat pocket and unlocks the door to one of three storage rooms, feels the hairs inside her nostrils freeze as she stares down the rows of half-empty shelves. The lights suspended from the snow-ceiling cast their flickering light on the snow-walls, waiting for her to choose.

*****

Birna cannot leave the island. There is no ice, no more land, for as far as she can see across the ocean's frigid turmoil of blue. And her legs are tired. Tired of walking from one end of the island to the other for days and days, finding only polar willow and patches of moss to eat. As Birna crests the mountain, she stares down at a hulk of something that glitters the way the ocean does during times of no-night. Her snout quivers with the smell of something living, something recently there. As Birna lumbers her wasting body down the barren slope, her fur glows yellow in the golden-armed sun.

*****

Deep within the vault, Silje's hunger wakes up. She recalls the last time she cooked a meal with fresh vegetables, fresh meat. Many seasons have passed since her kitchen was warm with the rich smell of lapskaus, the thick stew simmering on her stovetop, fogging the windows that framed the ever-looping dark. She closes her eyes and sees her husband's face, small droplets of stew in his beard, his smile a sliver of light. As the months redoubled, there were no more vegetables, nothing left to hunt, no fish left to catch. Silje has been the only one in town for some time now. Her empty house is filled with empty cupboards, empty cans. A dwindling pile of items she can burn to heat the stove. The memories gnaw at Silje, eating at her from the inside out. She opens her eyes, can almost hear the seeds murmuring to her from their neatly-stacked boxes and bins. She drags a mittened hand across the base of her nose and slowly makes her way between two sets of towering shelves.

*****

Birna grows thin as the sunlight grows thin. Two weeks ago, she wandered the streets of the little town, neat rows of colorful houses watching her with vacant-window eyes. She found only one scraggly dog wandering alone, too weak to run away from her as she charged. When she held the limp dog's skull between her jaws, took her first bite of meat in months, it was as if Birna could hear the barking echo in her ears, could taste the sour human breath drifting across canine shoulders, canine tails. Birna pulled against the unfamiliar pressure of the harness around her neck and shoulders, listened to the crunch and glide of the sled gaining on her in the shadowed not-night. And then, there on the frigid wind, she caught the faint scent of something else living, something with breath that coiled in the air. But when Birna lifted her head from the reddened fur and looked around her, only the silent town looked back.

*****

It is against Silje's nature to steal the seeds. She has been tasked with safekeeping them for so long. The seeds were meant for bigger things. For humanity's persistence and salvation. Somewhere on these shelves are seeds that survived the siege of Leningrad many, many decades ago. Scientists gave their lives for those seeds before they were relocated to the vault. Protected them from the German army, from their own hungry neighbors. The scientists' starving bodies went rigid surrounded by bags of rice they steadfastly guarded, refused to eat. On the shelves of the vault, seeds from North Korea rest near seeds from the South. Russian seeds next to American seeds. In the outside world, cooperation came too late. The forests burned. The oceans rose. Blackened air, toxic earth. Silje thinks of her twin daughters, born so little, so sick. Though many years have passed—so many that her hair is threaded with silver and white—she still remembers their bodies, small and warm among the tubes and machines. She remembers their tiny fingers wrapped around her husband's pinkie, around her thumb. Silje looks up at the arched permafrost ceiling, around at the curving permafrost walls, and sees her daughters in the incubator, where the nurses placed them together for comfort. Their heads were always turned toward one another. Each one held in the other's struggling gaze.

*****

Birna approaches the shimmering hulk cautiously, startles at her broken reflection in the mirrored roof, but does not shy away. She makes her way down the rocky slope, the ache in her belly driving her toward the first fresh scent in days. On the road outside the vault is a flat-legged thing, its skeletal form vacant and still. Birna sniffs at it, but it is not the thing that is alive. She raises her head, draws the lingering scent in. The smell outside the closed doors of the vault is not the familiar smell of reindeer. Though she has not eaten a reindeer in many months, Birna remembers. Reindeer smell like beasts made of growing things, their breath sweet with lichen and sedge. Their taste used to make Birna's head feel heavy, as if branches were sprouting from between her ears as her snout dipped deeper into their heated flanks. Instead, the vault smells like the ghost of the town. Though she has not seen a human for a long, long time, she remembers how they smell. They smell like the earth, but not the earth. The vault is like the ocean. She knows that somewhere inside is a creature that will eventually need to surface. Birna sits outside the door and waits.

*****

Silje has grown used to being alone. The others have all left, or died, and last winter her husband succumbed to an illness that swept through the town with rapid ferocity. Though so many abandoned the island, Silje had insisted on staying to manage the vault, to accommodate the increased requests for withdrawals. And then, those visits ended like so many other efforts had ended. Now, no more planes land with seed collectors and supplies. No more boats navigate the archipelago and its shrinking masses of land. All methods of communication collapsed, first into static and then silence. Silje lost all contact with the world beyond the island. She tries not to imagine what might have befallen everyone, everything, outside these isolated shores. She goes on living, goes on caring for the seeds. The seeds must be ready in case someone—anyone— comes back. Silje moved herself into the smallest house on the highest ground. The summers had been growing warmer for many years, and this past summer was the warmest yet, permafrost melting and flooding large swaths of the island. Deep inside the vault it is still cold and dry. The seeds will not grow on the island, among rocks and ice. But the island has nothing else to offer now, save for the seeds. At night, the first hint of winter holds Silje's little red house in its arms. The coal plant is deserted. When the snow comes, everything will be buried. Silje stands before the rows of seeds, trusting that their carefully tended lives can somehow save her own.

*****

Birna's body, even when hungry, is built for patience. When still-hunting on the ice, she waits for her prey to come to her. Her body knows how to go for weeks and weeks without food, feeding on itself. Sitting outside the door to the vault, Birna remembers the three un-lonely years when she was a mother. It has been a very, very long time since she has seen another bear. But her memories are patient, too. They allow themselves to be carried through wind and snow, through everlasting night, and they come to her when she is still, and waiting. First, the little bear-beginnings floated inside Birna while her body fattened up and the seasons turned. She came to this island as the dividing cells landed themselves at her core, burrowed in, and began to grow. She ate seals, and reindeer, and once a walrus that rippled and creased her skin with every swallow. Her lungs expanded with the strength of its bellow. She shook her head from side to side, tossed a long strip of hide across the ice, and reveled in the crash and groan of the fight. Inside the earthen den, snugged in by snow, Birna waited for her cubs. And once the cubs came, the three of them waited together for the winter to pass and the cubs to grow strong, their bodies curled into one another like milky dreams. Those years with her cubs, Birna felt that her body was three bodies, her belly three bellies, her heart three hearts. But her cubs have been gone many seasons now, and Birna knows she is the only heart left. The two cubs will never return to her, no matter how long she waits.

*****

Silje's hunger claws at her from within. She chooses a large plastic box from Burundi, hoping its contents will be something she can manage to eat. She has little chance of sprouting the seeds in her empty kitchen, of growing anything as winter brings its unending dark. So she imagines taking the seeds into her mouth, tasting their weight on her tongue. The box just fits within the span of her arms, and she hefts it onto an open section of shelf at the level of her waist. The barcode on the outside of the box tells her nothing about what might be within, so she does what she is forbidden to do. She uses her hunting knife to break the plastic seal and lifts the tight-fitting lid. Inside, neatly-labeled, silver packets and rubber-capped tubes nest in even rows. *Rice. Sorghum. Cowpea. Eggplant. Kidney beans. Plantains.* Silje imagines steaming platters and savory stews, though she knows that's not what she'll be able to make with these seeds. Instead, she'll swallow them one by one, wait for them to fill her fallow belly like a ripening field. Silje replaces the lid and hoists the box into her parka-bundled arms. She carries it gently, as if it were a child. A child she has been caring for and protecting for its many tender years. She opens the room's ice-kissed door and steps again into the tunnel, making her way back to what's left of the light.

*****

Each time a seal streaks toward the surface, Birna can sense it in her massive paws. Her jaws unlatch just a little. She salivates, anticipating the taste, the way her body will feel sleeker and swifter with every swallow. Her black eyes alert, the sea reflected in each lens. It is like that now, as Birna waits outside the vault. She can hear the measured footfalls drawing close. Can smell the earth-not-earth scent growing stronger within her powerful snout. The thorned thing in her belly turns over, needling at her from inside. Birna is unmoving, her thin and shaggy form poised to attack as the woman pushes open the door.

*****

When Silje opens the door of the vault, she sees not the sled, not the road, and not the waters of Isfjorden beyond. She sees the face of a polar bear, just two meters from her own. At first, she thinks the bear is a ghost. The ghost of her hunger, the ghost of what's left of the world. She has not seen a polar bear for many months, though once they roamed the island in the hundreds. Auroras of bears against showy polar lights. In the glacial seconds it takes for Silje to accept the very real body of this particular, unlikely bear, the beast has risen on its hind legs, doubling its height. Silje's heart is an iceberg, a cold blue rock in her chest. Her arms stiffen around the box of seeds. The bear's haggard body is like a building storm, an ice shelf cracking, collapsing as it crashes back to all fours and charges. Silje steps quickly backward and does the only thing she can think to distract the bear: she summons her strength and hurls the box of seeds at its open mouth. The heavy box shatters as it hits the ground, bursts into a hail of packets and vials around the startled beast as Silje slams closed the door.

*****

Birna shakes her head to clear the impact, stares at the closed door of the vault. She senses her prey is trapped. No vast ocean to hurtle away into, shadowing beneath the ice. Birna's patience is the kind hardened by failure and honed by eventual success. She can smell the earth-not-earth scent sharpening on the other side of the door. Birna is prepared to wait. She lowers her head to sniff at the strange items scattered around her, pushes at them with her dark-clawed feet. New scents tendril themselves into the black caverns of her nostrils, call to the thorned thing within. She flays the shiny-skinned objects with her teeth, crushes the slender not-eggs beneath her paws, and the seeds spill onto the frozen ground. She laps them up with her inky tongue, feels them spiraling down the length of her throat. She sways as an odd warmth begins at her snout and spreads across the arch of her spine. Birna's back rises in a landscape of hills, her skin sweats with the lush pulse of equatorial green. An unfamiliar blooming overtakes her body, and she sits back on her haunches, drunk with sprouting, dizzy with fronds and leaves. Birna is landlocked, river-swept. Her eyes begin to blur, and the vault disappears in a forest of clouds.

*****

It is against Silje's nature to kill a polar bear, one of the planet's few remaining sacred beings. But living here, at the crown of the Earth, Silje's heart has accepted its beaconing, its will to survive. Resting one hand against the steel door of the vault, she catches her breath, watches as it forms and reforms in the numbing air. The vault was built for short, efficient visits. For deposits and withdrawals. Not for hunkering down. The cold is deepening in Silje's body. She cannot wait inside the vault for as long as the bear can wait outside. She removes her mittens and reaches one hand over her shoulder, to where a rifle is slung across her back. Though she cannot remember the last time she saw a bear or any other living creature, she has not broken the habit of always being prepared. No one on the island would ever venture out unarmed, even if the only fanged thing they had seen for months was the sun. Silje knows the bear will not leave her. She can hear it shuffling and rummaging on the other side of the vault. When it goes quiet, she readies herself, and readies the gun. Balancing the rifle carefully, she slowly tilts her foot against the base of the door to nudge it into motion. No breath hovers before her lips. Then Silje kicks hard and casts the door wide.

*****

When the vault door opens, the earth-not-earth smell rushes into Birna's nose, pummeling the fevered haze of the seeds. She rights herself easily, swings her head side to side as she weighs her strategies, the sure way, this time, to take down her prey. She holds the human's eyes with her own, measures the human's steady gaze against the gnawing hunger at her body's core. When Birna lunges forward, she feels the ocean lift her limbs, feels herself vaulting the waves. But then comes a sound like icebergs colliding, and the pain explodes in her chest. As she thunders to the ground at the human's feet, the cold begins along her spine, where it presses against the open door. Birna hears herself moan, a rough, exhausted sound that spills down her tongue, past her teeth. As the pulsing of her body lessens, she remembers how it was when her cubs came. Alone in her den, she strained against the rhythmic throes. When the cubs finally slid from her body, she licked and licked them until they emerged from their cauls, their faces searching for the warmth of her side. Now Birna opens her mouth wide, calling out for those two hearts in the dark.

*****

Silje winces at the echo of rifle fire rebounding through the empty slopes. The bright stain of blood on the thick, white fur beside her boots looks to Silje like the flare that will certainly come at the end of the world. She nudges at the bear's side with the tip of the rifle, but the animal has gone still. Shaking, she sets the gun on the ground and crumples beside the bear's open mouth. She touches her forehead to the place between its unflickering eyes, cups her hands gently at the base of its jaws. Then she sits for a while against the propped-open door of the vault, the motionless creature beside her drenched in blue-gold light. The bear is too large for Silje to move on her own, so at last she unsheathes her hunting knife and kneels between its massive paws. This bear's pelt will keep Silje warm when the darkness comes. She'll store its meat in the frozen rooms of the vault, enough to survive the winter and face whatever remains when the sun returns. In her little red house that evening, Silje will take the first morsel of the bear's flesh into her mouth, and her limbs will pulse with a calm patience, an unfailing strength. She'll close her eyes, and her heart will spin. She will see a flurry of seals racing beneath her as she walks between mountains of snow. She'll feel the ice under her feet, buoying her across an expanse of blue. And there, at the top of the world, will be her daughters. Her little twin cubs. Two beings with their bodies curled close together, reaching for each other across the long night.

Flight Path

After three grackles and one red-winged blackbird smacked into our windows and a Canada goose fell dead from the sky into the middle of our backyard, Pen started building the nest. It was just before the 4th of July. I was stretched out in the porch hammock, half watching Pen drag broken branches, clumps of ivy, and tendrils of Himalayan blackberry bushes across the yard and half reading *The Lion, the Witch, and the Wardrobe.* I'd been re-reading *The Chronicles of Narnia* every summer since I was eight—something I'd always looked forward to, even after I was supposedly too old for them.

I had gotten my driver's license on the last day of school, which fell on my sixteenth birthday. I've never liked to be the center of attention, so my parents simply took me and Pen out for ice cream sundaes, and then I got to drive everybody home. I started my summer job the next day, assembling ethnically nonspecific fusion tacos in a food cart pod a couple of miles from our house. It got hot in the little food truck, and I spent every shift in a tank top with my hair bunched in a knot on top of my head. I worked evenings, the pod jumping with locals and tourists. Strings of café lights crisscrossed overhead, live music mingled with conversations, and a big fire pit blazed in the middle of it all. Before my shifts, I hung out with Pen while our parents were at work.

Pen had recently asked the rest of us to call them Pen and not Penelope or Penny anymore. So—despite my parents' initial reluctance—we buried Pen's birth name six feet under, and my little sister became simply my younger sibling, instead. Pen was eleven, going on twelve. They were dressed in their go-to outfit of a loose black t-shirt and cargo shorts. In our dad's leather work gloves, their hands looked ridiculously large. As Pen raided the overgrown foliage of our yard, their unruly curls were plastered to the sides of their face in the heat.

I peeked over the top of my book, in which Lucy had just tumbled back out of the wardrobe after visiting Narnia for the first time. "Pen, what's with the giant nest? You expecting a pterodactyl to move in?"

"Ha, ha, Greta, you're hilarious, no." Pen held a fistful of shrubby sprigs from our mother's massive rosemary bush. The dense, woody plant was almost as old as me, and with its riot of blue flowers and happy bees, it nearly dwarfed Pen's petite form.

Pen had a thing for birds long before they started dying in our yard. And this wasn't the first nest, either. Starting at about seven years old, Pen would gather up pipe cleaners, hair from our brushes, and embroidery floss used for the many friendship bracelets they wore to the point of unraveling, and I'd watch them weave the strands in and out of twiggy bits. Pen would line the nests up along their bedroom windowsill, the window open just a few inches, and wait for the birds to move in. Which they never did.

But this time felt different. Pen had been sullen since school let out, and I couldn't tempt them with any of the ideas I had come up with for activities. Walk to the park? No. Bake cookies? No. Create our own comic book? Still no. I had finally given up trying. But today, Pen was content, hyper-focused.

I shifted sideways in the hammock to survey Pen's work. This nest was on the ground, centered on the spot under the apple tree where grass wouldn't grow. Over the course of the afternoon's construction it had expanded to cover a sizeable portion of our tiny backyard. I guessed it was at least six feet in diameter now, sprawling away from the arborvitae hedge into the space between the flower beds and a dense cluster of ferns.

"Just don't sacrifice Mom's calla lilies for the cause," I warned.

That got me a big eyeroll.

"I'm not an idiot." Pen squatted and wove the rosemary into the growing ring. "And it's not a nest."

"It *looks* like a nest."

"Nests are for living in. This is a way station."

Pen momentarily lost their balance and tipped awkwardly onto their hip, then righted themselves into a squat again. "A way station?" I tried to recall what I knew about the concept, something about a place to stop on a journey. Mostly it made me think about railroads. Certainly not nests. "Where did you learn about those?"

"Read about them somewhere." Pen was a voracious reader, though they wouldn't read the Narnia books with me anymore.

"Huh." I thought of Lucy in the wardrobe, the rows of coats giving way to a forest draped in snow. "And who exactly are you expecting to stop by?" I teased. "Bigfoot?"

More eye rolling.

"No. It's for the birds." Pen had turned serious now, pushing dirt against the inside walls of the nest. "Where's the hose? The ground is too dry. I need to fill in these gaps."

Amused, I swung my legs over the side of the hammock and set my book down in its folds. "I think it's in the garage. Just a sec." A testament to our parents' many whims and unfinished projects, the garage was crammed with tools, old furniture, and thrift store finds that had once been intended to become something else but now only prevented us from parking our car inside. I wrestled the hose from a jumble of garden implements and dragged it behind me like a deflated python to where Pen was trying to sculpt the sides of the nest. "Here, I'll go hook it up." I handed Pen the bare end of the coil.

"Just a trickle, k? I only need a little mud."

I caught a flicker of memory, of a time when we were younger, and Pen would walk circles around and around the wading pool like a dog getting ready to lie down, mesmerized by the sun-sparkled water. I would inevitably convince them to fill the pool with dirt and sticks and flowers, and we'd end up so muddy that Dad would have to spray us down before letting us back in the house.

I turned on the hose the tiniest bit and waited for the water to make its way through the semi-kinked loops. "Why do the birds need a way station?"

"So they have somewhere to rest before they move on." Pen dribbled water along the inner curves of the nest, swirling the dirt into a goopy paste. "That's enough, Greta."

I tightened the spout until it squeaked off and wiped my wet hands on my shorts as I headed back toward the porch. "Like migrating birds? Do they do that in summer?"

"Yeah, if they're leaving a place where it's winter." Pen knew a lot about birds. Field guides were their favorite reading material, followed closely by a series of graphic novels about a quirky, supernatural summer camp for teenage girls. "But it's not for them. It's for the other birds, the dead ones."

"What?" I stopped halfway back to the hammock. "But we buried those. And anyway, hopefully there won't be any more."

"There will be, though." Pen looked up at me, their body suddenly seeming too big to be playing in a mud puddle in the backyard. "And they need a way station." Pen's eyes were steady, as deep green as our leafy summer trees.

They were starting to unsettle me. "That doesn't make any sense, Pen. Those birds were just a coincidence." I tried to sound authoritative. "Maybe our windows were too clean. Or, you know, they got sick from the pollution or something."

Pen shook their head at me and bent down to concentrate on shoring up the walls of the nest, careful as any good mason.

I sighed. What harm could it do, really, to let Pen keep building? At least they weren't sulking or in their room with the door closed anymore. I started toward the hammock again, and the promise of losing myself in a place where people really could talk to animals.

That's when I heard the branches crack above us, leaves rustling and scattering to the ground. Then a flurry of white feathers came crashing through our apple tree and landed in a heap right in the middle of the nest.

"Pen, get back!"

But Pen stayed where they were, squatting beside the nest, eyes on the bird. I grabbed a shovel that was leaning against the side of the house and approached warily.

Pen had always had an overactive imagination, spinning stories to themselves for hours on end. The kind of kid who invents invisible friends and pretends to talk to ghosts. And now, it seemed, birds. But lately Pen had become someone teachers and relatives tilted their worried heads at. Why didn't they like school anymore? Why didn't they want to hang out with their friends? In this moment, though, Pen looked oddly at ease.

"Don't freak out, Greta. It's dead."

I peered over Pen's shoulder. The bird looked like a crow, except it was almost completely white. And definitely a goner. Just a lump of feathers ruffling slightly in the summer breeze. I was still standing over the nest with the shovel slightly raised, like I was ready to play whack-a-mole. "What the heck is happening around here?"

"First visitor to the way station. I guess it's working."

I poked the crow with the tip of the shovel, just a little nudge.

"You're not sad? You don't think it's weird that birds keep dying in our yard?"

Pen shrugged. "It's safe here." They stood up and wiped their muddy chin with the corner of their t-shirt. "Put the shovel down, Greta. It's ok."

Pen talking like a grownup was freaking me out even more than the dead bird. "What's so safe about our yard in particular?"

Pen was looking down at the crow with a tender kind of calmness. "The world can't see them back here." Pen sounded very matter-of-fact. "They can rest until they're ready to change."

As I stared at the lifeless bird, curiosity started to win out over Hitchcockian horror. "Change into what?" I studied Pen. Their dirty face and chin-length curls. Their deep green, newly complicated eyes.

Pen's voice grew quieter, their head drooping down toward their small feet.

"Into whatever they want."

I thought of Aslan, the great lion of Narnia, lying dead on the stone table where he'd been slain by the White Witch and her followers. How they'd shaved his mane, tied down his strong paws. How, after everyone had left him, little mice came and nibbled through the ropes, freeing the lion even in his death. And how, impossibly, when no one was looking, the table cracked and the lion vanished, then returned even more beautiful, more powerful than before.

I lowered the shovel and leaned on its handle, balancing my chin on top of my interlaced hands to get a better look at the bird. The crow's head was twisted at an odd angle, its beak and eyes open. Black eyes that stood out like shiny buttons against the pale feathers. "Why aren't its eyes red?" I asked. "Isn't it albino?"

"It's leucistic."

I was impressed with Pen's ten-dollar vocabulary word. "What's that mean?"

"Partial loss of pigmentation. It can cause white skin and feathers. Doesn't affect the eyes, though." Pen was standing with their arms crossed now, hands in armpits, considering the crow. They stood like that a lot lately, covering up the little nubs rising on their chest.

"Did you learn that from a field guide?"

"YouTube. I've seen crows with light feathers in the neighborhood before. The other birds don't want to be around them. They're vulnerable. They stand out." Pen kicked gently at the side of the nest with one muddy-sneakered toe.

"Well, that's crummy," I said. I wanted to reach over and pull Pen's curls away from their sweaty cheeks, but I didn't.

"Yeah. I've never seen one all white like this, though. It's pretty, huh? Like an angel or something."

Our family wasn't religious in the least. I remember when I found out that the story of Aslan was supposed to be the story of Jesus, I was devastated.

"An angel?"

Pen made a small, impatient sigh. "I didn't say it *was* an angel. If it was, it wouldn't need a way station, would it? It just *looks* like an angel. Except for that broken neck." Pen uncrossed their arms and took me by the elbow, guiding me backward. "We should look away so it can move on."

"What? On to where?"

"Wherever's next."

It was getting late, and our parents would be home soon. "Pen, we should bury it like the others, before the neighborhood cats get to it. Or the raccoons or possums or whatever."

Pen stared at me with uncanny authority. I felt the age gap closing between us.

If I concentrate hard enough, I can still remember the moment when Pen was born—in a tub that the midwife had set up in our living room. Dad sat behind Mom in the tub while I watched from the couch with my Gramma, who held me on her lap as I clutched my beloved stuffed lion (I was destined to fall for Aslan from an early age).

Most of the memory is a blur, though I know my Gramma was talking calmly into my ear and stroking my hair, and I was so excited I thought I might combust. I was trying not to blink, afraid I'd miss it. My parents had explained that my baby sister would come out of Mom's belly underwater but that she wouldn't drown, and I was convinced that meant she would be a mermaid. What I do remember clearly is my dad lifting Pen out of the bloody water, all kicking legs and definitely no fishy tail.

But that was just the start of Pen showing me what they were not. Not a mermaid. Not a baby sister. Not a girl. They'd always had the ability to turn my world on its end, and most of the time I didn't want it to right itself again.

Most of the time.

I was staring back at Pen, ready with the shovel. "I'll dig a hole by the others."

"You don't need to do that, Greta. Just wait a few minutes. You'll see." Pen squinted through the late afternoon sun, clearly disappointed in me. It was a look I didn't want to have earned, and it almost stopped me. But I pulled myself together and headed for the corner of the backyard opposite the nest. Pen turned their back on the dead bird and watched me go, crossing their arms again while I dug. Sweat beaded and then rivered at my temples as I forced the hard ground to open into a crow-sized hole.

When I came back across the yard, Pen still had their back to the nest and was eyeing me with pre-teen satisfaction. They stepped aside as I headed toward the nest with the shovel, ready to scoop up the carcass and be done with it so I could lose myself in Narnia again. But the nest was empty. No broken-necked, white-winged, leu-whatever crow. I spun on Pen.

"Where did you put it?" It came out angrier than I meant it to. Pen's smugness fell from their face in lopsided surprise, like a scoop of melty ice cream dropping from its cone.

"Nowhere, Greta. I didn't touch it."

"Then where is it? Don't tell me it magically came back to life and flew away?" My sarcasm hovered in the heat of the summer air, thick and ugly.

"I didn't move it anywhere." Pen stood their ground, despite the tears starting to crest in their evergreen eyes. "It just moved on."

"Right. Pen, birds carry diseases. We need to bury it. Where is it?" I heard the adult-ness, the parent-ness, creeping into my older sister voice like an unwelcome guest.

"You don't believe me about the way station." Pen uncrossed their arms to wipe their eyes with the backs of our dad's leather work gloves.

Where had my belief in magic gone, anyway? Wasn't that why I kept reading the Narnia books over and over again? To hold on to it for as long as I could? And here I was, just like Lucy Pevensie's siblings, not believing a lick of what she told them about the lamppost, and the snow, and the very nice faun she had met in the land through the wardrobe, even though they had never, ever known Lucy to tell a lie.

I wanted for Pen to have the power to create a landing place between life and death. Just like I had wished for so many childhood years for the land of Narnia to be real. And maybe I should have let them have this one harmless deception. But Pen was nearly twelve, headed for middle school where the girls would be mean and the boys would be meaner and maybe there wouldn't be anyone else like my little non-mermaid sibling. I put the shovel down and looked Pen in the eyes. Pen with their dirty t-shirt and boy-shorts and too-big, muddy gloves.

"Magic's not real, Pen," I said. Something in me shattering, piercing the walls of my chest. "Show me where you put the crow."

Pen's face wavered, then hardened. They turned away from me toward the house, slipped the gloves off and let them fall onto the ground. "Go back to your book, Greta." Their voice barely audible over the slam of the screen door.

My heart felt as if it were liquifying, sliding down over my bones to pool in my toes. I walked to the nest, looked down into its muddy, empty center. Empty except for a single white feather caught on a blackberry bramble, stark and accusatory in the bright, bright onslaught of sun.

*****

That night the food carts were particularly busy. June's indecisive weather had finally morphed into July's perfect summer evenings—no sweatshirt needed, sandals out of the back of the closet. Around the fire pit, a large crowd happily munched on fancy grilled cheese sandwiches, artisan pizza slices, and vegan Buddha bowls to the accompaniment of an all-ukulele quintet. I was assembling tacos at lightning speed, my fingertips slippery with guacamole and kimchi. It was all so over-stimulating, there shouldn't have been room for anything else to rattle around in my head. But I couldn't stop thinking about Pen and the nest.

I hadn't been able to find the white crow.

I had looked all over the yard—front and back—through the garage, inside the mailbox, peeked over the neighbors' fence. No crow. When Mom and Dad got home, I just changed and headed out to work, leaving them to sort out Pen's mood. I had no idea if Pen would tell our parents about the way station, or the crow, or what a rotten sister I really was.

My best friend Lauren worked evenings with me, prepping cabbage and restocking the chicken, pork, and carnitas bins as fast as we could empty them. Lauren lived a few blocks away from us, so I snuck in my question between filling taco shells.

"Hey, have you had any birds in your yard lately? Like, dead ones, maybe?"

Lauren looked at me sideways, swapped out another bin. "You mean other than the decapitated ones our cat leaves on the doorstep?"

"Ew, Lauren. Bad kitty." I snuggled three chicken tacos together on a paper plate and passed them forward to the owner, who was working the window.

"Yeah, well, that's what cats do. Why? Do you have dead birds in *your* yard?"

I considered how much to tell her.

"Yeah, we've had a few birds fly into our windows recently. And a dead goose fell into the yard." It sounded like the setup for a mediocre Netflix horror series.

"Whoa! A goose? Like, it was flying over your house and just died in mid-air?"

It sounded even more ridiculous when Lauren said it back to me.

"I guess. I don't know. I thought maybe it was happening in the rest of the neighborhood, too." Two pork tacos, dollops of slaw, extra kimchi.

"Maybe it's the fireworks."

"What, like the noise is scaring them to death or something?" Folks on our block got started early with 4th of July celebrations every year, no matter the weather or laws. Booms and sizzles and pops for days leading up to the holiday.

Lauren shrugged. "Maybe. Birds seem like fragile things, don't they? All those hollow bones? Maybe they have little heart attacks. Hand me that empty carnitas bin, will you?"

Little heart attacks. I pictured the red-winged blackbird that had flown into our window. A mess of red and yellow feathers splayed atop a heap of shiny black. Tiny shattered skull, curled and knotted bird feet. Somewhere inside a tiny heart going still inside a thin basket of ribs. Pen and I had stood over its broken body, and I wondered how it had lost track of the sky and found us, instead.

*****

Having worked late at the pod the night before, I slept in the next morning, waking long after our parents had left for work. From my bedroom window, I could see Pen in the backyard, sitting in the nest and staring down into their lap. Pen's back was to me, the late morning light falling through the apple tree and onto their slumped shoulders.

Pen was probably still angry with me. As I looked for my flip-flops, I shuffled words of apology around in my head. *I'm sorry I accused you of lying?* But hadn't Pen been dishonest? Where had the crow gone? *I'm sorry I made you angry?* But hadn't I just been trying to prepare Pen for the harsher world outside of our backyard? *I'm sorry I wanted to bury the bird?*

Slowly, I pushed the screen door open and stepped out into the already-hot morning of the third day of July.

"Pen?" The door clattered shut behind me.

"Shhhhhhh." Not a hiss, not a command. Just a quiet, uncomplicated request.

I dropped my voice to a whisper. "Pen, are you ok? I just wanted to say…"

"Shhhhhhh. Greta, come and see."

There wasn't a hint of anger or resentment in Pen's voice. Only a kind of conspiratorial wonder, like when we were younger and our parents would take us out to the coast and let us run ahead of them down long stretches of sand to the tidepools. We'd carefully pick our way across the rocks, trying not to crush a single limpet or barnacle as we searched for sea stars and miniature crabs. We waggled our fingers above the pools, and the anemones waved their blue and green tentacles back.

I approached Pen slowly, stepped into the circle of the nest. "What do you have?" I crouched down behind them. Pen was holding something small and shiny in the bowl of their palms.

"Hummingbird," whispered Pen. "I found it on the ground under your window. It's still breathing, but it's letting go."

I pictured the tiny bird hovering at my bedroom window, watching me sleep. Imagined the blur of its body, the thrum of its wings. Maybe it had been drawn to something blooming in my dreams. Something I could no longer remember. I considered the possibility that being held by a human was more traumatic for this delicate being than dying alone in the grass. But something about the way Pen cradled the bird—full of reverence, not stroking it or speaking to it but just witnessing its slowing breaths—made me hold my tongue.

"She's beautiful," I said quietly, settling down beside Pen, my arm just barely pressing against their shoulder.

"He," Pen corrected. "*He's* beautiful." Proper use of pronouns had become increasingly important to Pen. Even in the case, apparently, of animals. The bird's iridescent feathers glowed orange, like the copper of a lucky penny glinting on the sidewalk. Pen's voice was calm and even. "Sometimes I wish I was a bird," they said.

"So you could fly?"

Pen tilted their head up at me for just a moment, their eyes sad but not tearful, and then looked back down at the bird.

"No. So I could wear colorful feathers. Show them off. But not in the body of a girl."

From somewhere down the street came the staccato popping of snappers being thrown against the ground. The hummingbird twitched, then went still.

"I'm sorry, Pen," I said. The simplest of apologies sifted out of my mouth, trying to mean everything. Sorry for the death of the pretty little bird, for being an unkind sister, for not knowing how to help Pen molt into a body they wanted to be in.

"Close your eyes, Greta," they said.

So I did. I closed my eyes and felt the heat of the sun on my face, turning the insides of my eyelids as orange as the bird's shimmering body.

"Now put out your hand."

And I did, something rekindling within my ribs. I stretched one hand out in front of me, eyes still closed. My breath paused in my body as I felt Pen shift the dead hummingbird from their hands into my upturned palm. I sat completely still. The feathers were soft and warm, and the weight of the tiny body felt vital. Significant.

Beside me, Pen took my other hand. Pen's fingers were small and sweaty inside mine, and I held on more tightly, picturing the two of us running beside the rhythmic roar of waves. I could feel the hummingbird's little beak resting against my thumb, and then a lightness, as if I were holding a cloud. When Pen let go of my hand, I opened my eyes. Pen was smiling at me with their green, green eyes as I looked down at my two empty palms.

*****

The food carts didn't shut down for the 4th of July. If anything, they were even busier, folks catching a bite to eat before heading downtown to see the big fireworks display on the river. Lauren and I chopped and restocked and filled and plated a mile a minute, in time with the hipster marching band parading around the pod in spangled costumes and stilts. Finally, after hours of an endless line of people outside our cart, darkness came on and the pod started to empty out. Lauren and I took a break by the fire pit and watched the stream of cars and buses and bicycles making their way toward the river. I thought of my family at home. For the first time this year, Pen didn't want to go to the fireworks.

The carts were only a few blocks across the river from downtown, and as the display started up, we could see the colors bursting and streaking over the city. I had told Lauren about the crow and the hummingbird, but not about how they had vanished. I couldn't explain, couldn't put into words, the feeling of the bird's tiny, lifeless body lifting from my hand.

"Any new dead birds today?" she asked.

"Not today," I said. It had been a quiet afternoon with Pen holed up in their room, probably watching YouTube videos. They wouldn't let me come in. I had tried to read but was too distracted, my imagination bouncing between the waiting nest (Was it waiting? What was it waiting to receive?) and Pen's shuttered room. Their door closed. Their window not even open a crack, despite the heat. Silence on the other side.

I turned toward Lauren. "I'm kind of worried about Pen."

Lauren looked at me sympathetically. "They'll be ok. They're such a cool kid. Remember the time we were studying together for that big math test and they made us Play-Doh cupcakes for luck and insisted we had to eat one bite each or we wouldn't pass?"

I nodded. It wasn't just with birds. Pen had always been empathetic, always kind.

Lauren smiled and continued. "I bet they'll find their people in middle school. People who'll accept them. The real them. You'll see. We found each other, didn't we?"

"Yeah." I leaned into Lauren, then away again. "This feels different, though. I don't know how to help."

"Just keep being there for them," she said. "Dead names and dead birds and all."

The sky was loud with color and sound. Inside my chest, my heart felt hollow and dark. Only an empty wardrobe where there used to be the magic of snowy, lamplit woods.

*****

When I got home, mini-explosions of firecrackers were still going off up and down our street. Despite the nonstop noise, my parents' room was dark and humming with their soft snores. But the door to Pen's room was uncharacteristically open. I poked my head inside, just a hint of moonlight spilling in from the window. Their bed was empty. I checked the bathroom, the living room, the kitchen. No Pen. Just when I was beginning to panic and starting to consider waking up my parents, I saw that the backdoor was ajar, the screen creaking back and forth on its hinges in the late-night breeze.

As I stepped out onto the porch, the yard came into focus in the smoky, firework-flared light. All around me, crackles and whistles and pops filled the air, threaded with sirens and laughter and wailing dogs. And under the apple tree, an immobile form huddled in the center of the nest.

"Pen?" My voice a tiny squeak amidst the snaps and hisses and booms.

I hurried toward the nest and knelt beside Pen, who was lying curled into a fetal ball. I put my hand on their shoulder, shaking them. "Pen?"

A screeching sizzle overhead. And then Pen's small voice.

"I'm awake, Greta."

I sat down next to them, willing my heart to slow back down. "What are you doing out here?"

Pen sat up slowly, bits of twigs and dirt clinging to their matted hair.

"Waiting."

"Waiting for what?" One of Pen's hands was closed into a fist. I touched their tightly-clenched fingers. "What do you have there? Another bird?"

Pen shook their head, looked down toward their lap.

I scooted closer. "Let me see."

Reluctantly, Pen peeled back their fingers and opened their hand. In the cup of their palm, the red, white, and blue of perhaps a dozen Tylenol capsules. The kind from our parents' medicine cabinet.

My heart solidified in my chest. Somewhere down the street, an explosion set off a relentless, honking alarm.

Pen looked up at me, their face streaked with tears. "I didn't take any," they said, handing the pills over to me without meeting my eyes. I tucked them into my pocket carefully, like horrible magic beans. "I just brought them in case."

I could barely coax a whisper from my throat. "In case what?"

Pen looked up at the flashing, starless sky. "In case the way station didn't work for me."

I took Pen's empty hands inside mine. My little non-mermaid, my sweet sea star finder, my flightless, unmoored sibling. "Where were you trying to go?"

The car alarm chirped off, and the night was suddenly quieter, despite the chorus of whistles that still sang and fizzled all around us.

"You don't know what it feels like, Greta," Pen said quietly. "To be in the wrong body. I want to move on. To a new one."

When Aslan, the great lion, returned from the place beyond death, he'd walked through the witch's courtyard, where all the brave Narnian creatures had been turned to stone. He'd breathed his warm, living breath upon each statue, and one by one the creatures awakened back into their bodies. The beavers and rabbits, the fauns and dwarves, the centaurs with their horses' hooves and human hands. It was my favorite part of the story, all the land ringing with newfound voices.

"It's going to be ok, Pen," I said. Therapists and hormone treatments and bullies and our parents all smashed up against each other inside my head.

I gathered Pen into my arms. "I'll help you."

Pen relaxed against me, then lay down and put their head in my lap the way they used to do when they were little and we'd snuggle together in my bed while I read them stories. Fairytales and adventures, and, at their insistence, field guide entries about birds. Favorite habitats, shapes and sizes, songs and calls. Now, I stroked the side of Pen's face, ran my fingers through their tangles of curls.

"Will you cut my hair tomorrow, Greta?" they asked. "Short?"

I looked down at Pen's damp face, their barely open eyes eclipsing in the shadows. I didn't want to move. I was afraid that if I turned away, Pen might disappear.

"I will," I said.

"Ok," Pen murmured, pressing up against me in the wide, safe ring of the nest.

Around us, the darkness snapped and echoed, cacophonous and alight. I rested my hand on Pen's back, their shoulders rising and falling as they settled into sleep. And as I looked up into the apple tree, I was sure I saw the wild, sharp-eyed form of an owl swivel its head to look down at us before it lifted, open-winged and alive, into the noise of the night.

Suffer

My brother and I have been walking across the desert for many turns of light and dark. We walk rib to rib, so close that the yellow fur of our shoulders blends together, black spots merging when one of us stumbles and leans into the other for support. We separated from our mother some time ago, as is our way when cubs are old enough to hunt for themselves. It has been so long since our last meal, we barely remember the taste of impala, how the flesh felt against our rough tongues. This is the Namib, and orange sands shift around our paws. The vultures stalk us, circling. I am afraid the sun will eat us before we find a watering hole.

We are alone, Berriz and I, but we are not alone. The humans keep their distance, but we can smell them on the hot wind. They point machines with long noses at us, but we know the machines are not guns. We have seen guns before and have heard how they crack the air and echo out to the horizon. We have seen how sometimes, humans use guns to capture our kind, and we do not know where these unlucky ones are taken.

My brother was captured once, but he does not remember anything after he fell on his side in the dirt. The sun had just pulled the whole of its body into the sky when the humans came for him. I cried and cried, all day my voice like a wounded bird in the bush. He was returned just as the sun was bloodying the rim of our world, and I licked his face until he awakened. He wears a collar around his neck now, with a large bulge like a knucklebone at his throat, and the humans follow us wherever we go.

Danari. My name is a faint rumble in my brother's mouth. *I cannot go any farther, my brother.* Berriz's lean body is like a branch that splinters from its tree in a storm. He sits down on the blazing sand, and it seems that the spots on his back fade into the dust. His legs have grown thinner than mine, and it is hard to remember how, before this journey, we were so fast we could outrun all the other animals. Wildebeests, gemsboks, zebras, their stripes and horns and shaggy faces a blur as we sprinted after the herds, singling out the ones who fell behind. We would hunt together, our muscles strong, our bones slender and light as we raced across the veldt. Now, Berriz lowers himself onto his empty belly—empty as mine—and curls his long tail around his face to shade his amber eyes from the midday sun.

We have stopped, and so the humans have stopped, too. The mechanical beast they ride is many yards away from us, but I can hear it sigh and go to sleep. I hear the long-nosed machines in the humans' hands: click, spin, whirr, click. Like insects running from the pangolin's long tongue. The machines are pointed at us, and I think they replace the humans' inferior eyes. *Brother*, I say, *we must keep going.* I nudge my black-striped snout into his. I hear the wind lift the feathers on the vultures' wide wings.

But Berriz does not move. He does not answer me. After a hunt, we pant to cool our exhausted bodies with the bellows of our huge lungs. But Berriz is hardly panting at all. I have to press myself against him to feel the reassurance of his breath. *Brother*, I say again. The high pitch of my voice scurries across the expanse of desert, startles the humans and their lesser ears. Click, spin, whirr, click. *Let us walk a little more. We will find water. Let us not summon the vultures and their sunbaked skulls.* The voices of the humans drift to me through the shimmering air. I look up at them, away from Berriz. Why do they do nothing but stare?

Once, I saw a human collapse, his tall body crumpling to the ground. The other humans circled him, kneeling like lions around a kill. But no. They put their hands on him. They leaned their ears close, hovering above his mouth. They shouted and then lifted him from the earth. They led him to the shade and brought him water. I had seen how they care for their own, like our mother tended my brother and me.

But our mother is far away. It is me, and it is Berriz, and we are alone even though we are not alone. I nudge my brother again, but still he does not move. Why do the humans not help us? Can't they see that Berriz is unwell? I bark and chirp at them, calling the way we called for our mother when we were young. Do the humans not care if the creature who wears their collar lives or dies?

I lie down next to my brother and lick his face, but his eyes do not open. *Berriz!* I cry, my mouth against his mouth. But I cannot hear my brother's heart. I cannot feel his breath in my nostrils. A vulture lands on the sand, a few feet off. And then another, and another. I snarl, show them my teeth. They hop closer, bowing their red, wrinkled heads and fixing me with their black eyes. How can I leave my brother? But these birds tell me, this is the way of our world, of the Namib.

Click, spin, whirr, click. Will the humans stay to watch my brother turn to bones? If I walk away, they will lose me when the darkness comes. Thirst claws at my throat. But I cannot leave Berriz, even as the wings around us begin to hide the sun. I stare at the humans over the setting of my brother's body. How will I walk this desert alone?

Ichthyoforest

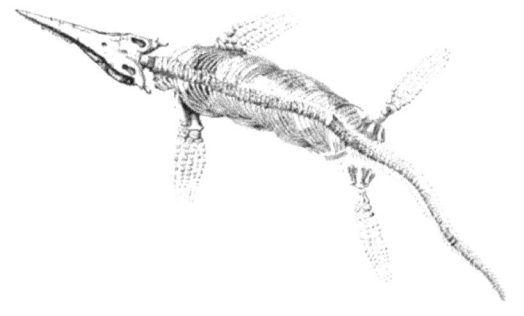

Myrna rounds the sea stack as the sky struggles to brighten through gray clouds. It's October, low tide, barely sunrise, and she has this stretch of coastline to herself, the tree-capped rock formation rising out of the sand beside her. She's still barefoot, sand between her toes, after wading through the shallow creek that divides the beach and splits at the stack's rocky base. The ocean is never warm here on the Oregon coast, even in summer, and her feet are nearly numb. But Myrna doesn't want wool socks or boots between her body and what awaits her just south of the creek.

Myrna feels invisible in the mist that has settled along the coast this morning. Her silver hair escapes in wisps from beneath her knitted cap, and her thin fingers hook into the collars of her boots, one in each wrinkled hand. She walks more slowly than she used to, but she's not slow. Her balance is steady, even as her feet sink into the water-logged sand. A lone seagull dips into her path and lands on the beach, tottering along in front of her as if leading the way. As she leaves the sea stack in her wake and walks after the bird, she strains her eyes until she can finally make out the silhouette of the ghost forest materializing in the dim light.

Myrna moved to this blip of a coastal town a few months back, leaving behind an ex-husband who had already left her and a daughter who forsook her before that. Myrna chose the town—if it could be considered a town at all—specifically for the ghost forest. She's one of perhaps 200 residents in cottages nestled into the hills, looking down on one lone restaurant and a general store along the highway. Myrna had a feeling about this place the first time she visited years ago and walked among the ancient, decaying tree stumps scattered across the sand. And then last summer, when she was all alone—standing paralyzed in her kitchen amidst the rubble of her marriage—she felt it calling her back. Myrna left her noisy city, her nosy friends, for this little town where she knew no one, where she could disappear along the line of the sea.

Across the span of beach, nearly a hundred stumps stand sentinel in the sand before her: barnacled phantoms in the autumn mist. Some are jagged and broken, while the tops of others have eroded to form bowls where small sea creatures await the return of the tide. Myrna is partial to the ones that look like faces, wizened and contemplative as they stare out toward the surf. Two thousand years they've been anchored here, their roots still buried in soil deep beneath the sand. Myrna walks into the middle of the remains of the great Sitka spruce forest, stops and turns to face the waves.

For years now, since about the time her husband stopped touching her, Myrna has been compiling a bestiary. It's a kind of diary, populated by unimpossible beings. Until recently, she hadn't actually seen any of the beasts, but she never doubted their existence.

Bigfoot. Bill and I went hiking on the Olympic Peninsula. Anywhere there might have been footprints, covered by leaves. I miss the way Alice used to hold my hand when she was little. I miss when Alice didn't want to let go. I miss Alice. If Alice had been hiking with us, she would have found the nests. The bigfoots make giant nests on the ground. Anthropologists have found them, but they won't tell anyone where. They study the nests, which are definitely not made by birds. Definitely not by humans. The bigfoots sleep in the nests, scientists can tell by the way the foliage is pressed down. Somewhere in that foliage, in the soil underneath, they will find something left behind. Maybe a bit of hair. I miss Alice's tangled hair. I miss how Alice would build blanket forts in the living room when she was small. She always invited me inside. I was too big, but I liked being in a too-small world with Alice. While we were hiking, I tried to tell Bill about the nests. They could have been anywhere around us, among the trees. Bill never believes me. Bill never wants to talk about Alice. We have forgotten how to build a world in which we can lie down together.

This morning, the wind is half-hearted. Myrna's cheeks feel raw from the cold, from the dampness of the mist, but she's not too cold to wait. Though Myrna only saw the sea creature once, floating among the truncated trees, swimming through the foggy air, she is hopeful it will eventually return. From its shape, at first she thought it was a dolphin. But its snout was too long, its jaws lined with too many teeth. Huge flipper-like limbs, eyes with large, round pupils that took no notice of her. Now, she's done her research, and she's sure of what she saw. A fish lizard. An ichthyosaur of the Mesozoic Era, when all of Oregon was covered by a shallow ocean.

Myrna has no qualms about the unexplainable. It's not really a question of belief. Unexpected things happen all the time. She has seen how someone who used to be your everything, your beloved, can turn away from you. Can turn out to be someone else entirely, like the selkies who unzip their animal skins to walk among humans on land. Myrna thinks that her husband must have been only pretending to love her, and now he's gone back to the sea. Another life. The one he kept from her for nearly ten years.

Mothman. What's the difference between a sandhill crane and a winged man in the dark? The wildlife biologist explained to the reporters that the birds are tall—almost as tall as a man— with huge wingspans and reddish markings around their eyes. That perhaps a crane strayed from its migration route, was taken for something it was not. What happens when a being loses its way? What happens when we happen upon something unrecognizable? When we were first married, Bill looked at me like I was a luna moth, silky and scented in the night. And he was gentle. Clear-eyed and open-armed. But now he is red-eyed in the darkness. No wonder the color of anger is hot and bright. He is something else now, trying to stay out of my sight.

Myrna first saw the ichthyosaur after moving into her new home. It was warm, late July. She was awake, tossing and turning to the sound of waves that should have been calming, shushing her body to sleep. She knew she shouldn't walk on the beach by herself at night, that the ocean with its sneaker waves and riptides can be an unpredictable companion. But she went anyway, picking her way down the path with the help of a full moon, no clouds. The tide was low, and when she reached the far side of the towering rock formation, the ghost forest spread across the expanse of beach before her like a silent, lonely vigil.

Myrna walked among the trees, stopping to pick up sand dollars and then replacing them. The moon lit the fronds of anemones in the eroded stump-bowls. Mussels clung to the sides of the spruce-ghosts, patient in the salty air. Myrna walked to the end of the ghost forest, then turned and leaned against one of the taller stumps to rest before walking back home. The moon hovered above the ocean, a luminous giant in the sky's crowded assemblage of stars. As Myrna plotted her return path through the ghost forest, something moved in the distance, low across the sand perhaps five yards off. Beyond, the sea stack's indistinct form climbed the sky. Myrna thought perhaps a seal had come ashore, was making its way back toward the bright line of waves. But it was large, at least twelve or thirteen feet long. And then she saw the tail, swaying back and forth as the creature navigated between trees. Saw the dorsal fin rising above the stumps. This was not an animal beached, a sea thing stranded. As Myrna took a step forward, daring for a closer look, the fish lizard plunged into the sand, its tail vanishing into a jumble of grounded kelp.

Myrna rushed forward and kneeled beside the huge pile of kelp. All these years, she had been waiting to see some fabled beast.

Now this being, too, had slipped away from her. She dove her hands into the kelp's slippery tendrils, but her fingers found only the wet disappointment of sand. She wrapped her arms about herself, tried to remember the last time she spoke to her daughter. Myrna was long past feeling guilty now. No matter how well you tended to someone, how much you showed up, they could still choose to run away.

Nessie. Every sighting sets off a tremor of hope. Today I thought I saw Alice at the Christmas tree lot. The same one we have gone to every year since she was small. Bill and I still go, but it isn't festive anymore. We don't know what to say to one another, so we just hurry our choice and get out of the rain. Scientists say the sea serpent has no biological basis. That the sightings are wishful thinking, misidentified mundane objects, hoaxes. I thought I would know Alice's neck anywhere. Would recognize the carriage of her shoulders, the funny way she tilts her head. It could have been her, pacing carefully among the rows of trees, inclining her head to judge their symmetry. Sometimes things appear bigger than they really are. Water beast, or Labrador fetching a stick? Monster, or otter spinning at the surface of the lake? I mistook the stranger for Alice. It's been three years since she left. Alice is a different kind of stranger to me now.

Since that night, Myrna has returned every time there is a tide low enough to reveal the ghost forest, at an hour when she's certain she'll be alone. She stalks the ancient trees, hoping the ichthyosaur will appear to her again. Now, as she reaches the first fractured stumps, she sets down her boots, smooths the damp folds of her jacket. She heads for her favorite of the ghost trees: the one that looks like a laughing face. Its top is rounded and furred in green algae. Two bumps partway down look like eyes, browed with barnacles. Below that, the stump is split by a deep notch, the kind a beaver might make to fell a large tree. Myrna imagines that beaver, gnawing away when the earthquake hit some three hundred years earlier and dropped the forest into the tidal zone. She pictures the ocean water rushing in, decapitating the trunks and burying them beneath mud. Perhaps burying the tree-feller, too.

Myrna likes the notched stump best not just because it survived the earthquake, the burial, the eventual unearthing when unusually powerful storms pummeled the coast and eroded away the sands to reveal the remains of the trees. Alice would have been about six or seven those winters. Not yet full of turbulence and lashing. No, Myrna loves this stump above the others because it also survived the devouring. It made of the notch a mouth. What's left of the tree laughs in the face of everything that tries to knock it down.

Months ago, when Myrna found out about her husband's affair, she felt herself split in half, falling. At that point, Alice had been gone a dozen years. Myrna had grown used to not knowing where Alice was. *If* she even still was. But this was another kind of not knowing. For close to a decade, Myrna's husband kept his secret from her. Myrna felt a fool. The woman had been her friend. Often came over for dinner.

Chupacabra. The beast is vampiric, feeds off the blood of others. Fanged. Clawed. Something about it, reptilian. Sometimes we would cook a meal together, she and I. She diced onions neatly, never shed a tear. Allicin. That's the substance released from onions that makes you cry. Allicin. Allicin. Alice. Sometimes she would talk to me about Alice, console me, tell me I had been a good mother. That I was not the reason Alice had been troubled. Not the cause of her running away. The goat-sucker pierces animals in the neck, drains all the blood from their bodies until their hearts are empty and still. Its eyes are large. It takes whatever it wants. Even if it's just an ordinary beast, even if there are explanations, the goats still pile up in lifeless heaps. The harm has already been done.

When Myrna reaches the laughing stump, she settles her body against it. Tries to settle her mind. The tide is far out, the beach strewn with the ocean's discardings. Alice would love this place. At least the young Alice would. Myrna imagines her running among the ghost trees, pail swinging in one hand and the other grasping a bright plastic shovel, hair whipping about her in the wind. She thinks even 16-year-old Alice would like it here, the broken Alice, the Alice who left. This place is a monument of beautiful, broken things. Alice is 30 now. If the world still houses Alice. Myrna is torn by two wishes. One, that Alice is alive somewhere, anywhere. Two, that Alice is not. Because Myrna cannot bear the thought that her daughter would not return to her, would leave her for good.

Myrna is lost in thought when the ichthyosaur emerges from the sea. Her mind clears instantly, and she stands up straight, keeps very still, her heart quickening in her chest. The creature hovers above the sand, rudders its long, gray body toward the ghost forest. Toward Myrna. It moves deliberately, much more slowly than it is capable of swimming. As if the air is more difficult to navigate than the water.

The huge marine reptile appears to be both there and not there. One moment it seems to Myrna that the beast is solid and real, its skin mottled, smooth length of its snout arrowing toward where she stands. The next moment, she can see right through its long body to the stumps on the other side. It fades and brightens, dissolves and resurfaces, as it continues to approach. It occurs to Myrna that perhaps the ichthyosaur is stalking her, predatory creature that it is. She tries to appear as un-fishlike, un-squidlike, as possible, tries to blend in to the sea-woolly stump beside her, its mouth ever-open, ever-laughing. She is afraid, but she does not turn and run. Alone here on the beach, the sky now blooming with streaks of pink and orange among the stubborn clouds, she is ready to greet whatever comes.

Jersey Devil. In some origin stories, it is an unwanted child. A cursed child, banished. Bipedal, it stands like a kangaroo. A chimera, the devil has the head of a horse or goat, the wings of a bat, arms with clawed hands, legs with cloven hooves, horns, a forked tail. Sometimes, I go entire days without anyone touching me. Before Bill and I slept turned away from each other, he used to reach out for me in the night, tucked me into the space between his arms. When Alice was little, she would cling to my legs, press her body into mine. I rubbed circles on her small back, used my fingers to untangle her hair. Is it the shunning that makes a body turn unfamiliar? Do the horns grow more twisted, the hands more gnarled, the longer they go untouched? And what about Alice? Was the mother in me so monstrous as to drive her off? What is happening to her body in the wide, unwelcoming world? Is she curled up, her heart hardened, or have her wings leathered and strengthened and carried her away? When I look at myself in the mirror now, there is no one behind me, hands on my shoulders, to ease the human ache in my skin.

The ichthyosaur has drawn itself alongside Myrna—who stands unmoving, arms relaxed at her sides—so close she can see every detail of its form. Its enormous eyes take her in, and it opens and closes its long mouth again and again, revealing a crowd of spiked teeth. It's an odd beast: such large eye sockets, bulge of belly, snout like a huge pair of needle-nose pliers. Myrna is filled with gratitude that it has come to her. She lifts her arm, reaches out her hand.

When Alice was born, the midwife placed her on Myrna's bare chest, skin-to-skin. The baby was warm and slippery, and Myrna laid one hand on Alice's back, cupped the other one around her tiny bottom. Such a strong and fragile thing, her baby. Myrna remembers her own body trembling, exhaustion and elation a murky tonic running through her veins. Bill knelt beside her, whispered to her, stroked her sweat-damp hair. His hand on top of her hand on top of the baby's body. And then Alice's voice, rising shrill and fierce and new into the room.

Myrna's body is trembling now, too. She half expects the ichthyosaur to vanish at her touch, but it is tangible, its smooth body cool and wet. She is eye to eye with the beast as it floats above the sand, and it allows her to run her hand down the length of its front fin. When was the last time she touched someone this intimately? That someone trusted and welcomed her touch? She imagines the fan of bones inside the beast's flipper, remembering the photos she's seen of the skeleton unearthed by Mary Anning, the great British fossilist, at the beginning of the 19th century.

Myrna pictures Mary at 12 years old, meticulously excavating an ichthyosaur's bones for months and months, bundled in wool on the frigid English coast. She knows that Mary was not recognized for her work at the time, that she was treated unkindly, called a fraud. She can only hope that the many creatures Mary found were a comfort to her, some sort of steadfast companions. As Myrna turns and places her other hand on the body of the ichthyosaur, sliding her fingers down its side to rest at the ridge of its dorsal fin, she imagines Mary's hands on the surfacing bones, lovingly coaxing them back into the visible world.

Loveland Frogman. What we encounter when we are by ourselves, in the dark, is no less real than the ordinary beings we walk among and converse with by day. When we slam on

our brakes, stare out into the beams of our headlights, we see
what we could not see before, when it was lurking on the
periphery. By the time Alice ran away, she was nearly
unrecognizable as my daughter. Her face did not look like her
face, dark circles around sunken eyes. Her skin did not look
like her skin, covered in lesions and track marks. The police
officer who sighted the Frogman said it stood up from a crouch,
then climbed over the guardrail and scrambled down the
embankment into the river, gone. When Bill left, I watched him
go. I was there while he packed. I was there when he walked
out the door and got into her car. I watched him drive away.
The forest is there, beside us. No matter how much we try to
keep to the road.

Standing beside the ichthyosaur, the ghost trees materializing more clearly all around her as the coastal mist dissolves, Myrna feels empty and full at the same time. Columns of sun now slice sideways through the clouds, but under her hands, the body of the ichthyosaur is fading. No longer solid beneath her grasp, its dorsal fin shimmers in the growing light, and then the fish lizard is in motion again, circling her, blinking its giant eyes, before it heads back toward the sea. Its undulating body becomes skeleton, becomes fossil, and Myrna finds herself running after it, into the returning tide. By the time the ichthyosaur disappears completely, Myrna is ankle deep in the freezing water, sobbing.

As she stands in the pull of the waves, sand sinking around the outlines of her bluing feet, the ground begins to shake. The tremors start small and quickly grow stronger, throwing Myrna off balance, and she falls onto her side in the surf. As the reality of the earthquake swells in her brain, Myrna knows she should get herself to higher ground. But something keeps her rooted, staring out at where the ichthyosaur vanished into the sea. She could just sit here, growing colder and colder, and let the ocean claim her, too.

Did anyone need her anymore? Though Bill hadn't really been hers for many years now, the thought of him as someone else's cleaves her heart in two. No, her heart had already cracked when Alice left. Where was Alice? Was she out there somewhere, wishing for a mother again? As the ground shifts and churns beneath her sopping body, Myrna looks back at the ghost forest. A few of the smaller stumps are toppling, but most hold fast. Her notched stump is laughing and laughing, jostling back and forth in the shuddering sand.

Then, all at once, the ground stills. A great roar rises up from the ocean, like some monster awakening in the deep. As the roar subsides, the sirens start up, blaring a looping wail that vibrates inside Myrna. She pushes herself to her hands and knees just as the waves retreat, receding farther and farther, revealing the seabed and stranding thousands of marine creatures in the trough. Something in Myrna ignites then. She stands quickly, backing away from the withdrawing ocean. Down the beach, the sea stack is a lonely colossus, the waters that normally lap at its back now frighteningly far from shore.

Myrna's mind swirls with the body of the ichthyosaur, the body of her not-husband, the somewhere-body of her daughter. Myrna knows that after the drawback of the ocean comes the surge of the tsunami wave. Seconds or minutes, there is no way to tell. But one thing is suddenly clear: she does not want to be taken. She does not want to be buried, swept into the frothing sea. She turns her back on the ocean and runs.

She stumbles through the ghost forest, using the stumps to propel herself forward. She does not look back, not wanting to see the shoaling wave. Myrna knows she cannot reach the end of the beach, will not be able to make it to the hills where her little house is safely tucked away. So she heads for the sea stack and the steep trail that leads up its side. Myrna's bare feet are so cold, her legs so stiff, it seems she is barely moving. The sea stack looks impossibly far away. The sirens resound in her ears. She has little time before the onrushing tide.

Just when she feels she might collapse, a sudden movement catches Myrna's eye, and the ichthyosaur is beside her, its body miraging in the rising sun. Through her mind, a flash of Bill tilting up her chin and leaning in to kiss her. A flash of Bill receding like the sea. She throws her arms around the ichthyosaur's neck, tries to hold on to its slippery form. A flash of Alice sleeping against her chest. A flash of Alice's bedroom, abandoned. Myrna is propelled forward, the sea stack drawing nearer and nearer. A flash of her own face, laughing. A flash of Alice standing at her door.

Over and Back

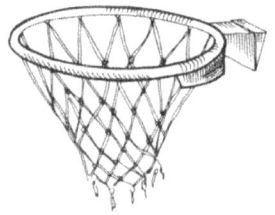

I can't see the angry waters of the Chesapeake Bay in the darkness, the wind bellowing around me like a banshee undone, but they've soaked me from the outside in, salty whitecaps sloshing sideways against my heart. Ropes of blond hair whip about my head, but I'm too drenched and battered to care. Here I am, standing in the boggy ground of the Uppards with headstones and arrowheads and the rusted remains of all manner of machines loosening beneath my feet, having it out with a hurricane.

Before this moment, all I wanted was to get off this island before it's eaten by the sea. I was born here, sluiced from one brackish home into another. In my seventeen years I've watched the ocean coming for us faster and faster, stealing our coastline by the acre, while the adults talk about politicians and seawalls, still thinking something can be done. But living here is like being invisible to the world, like we're already a bunch of ghosts. You couldn't pile up enough rocks along these shores to make any kind of life for a girl like me to look forward to. Before this moment, nothing to hold on to and the edges of my island drowning under relentless waves, I thought all I needed to save was myself.

I had a plan how to leave.

I want to be a referee, and I've set my sights on the NBA. The league's only got eight women refs so far, which tells you all you need to know about who still calls the shots in this world. I know the game even better than I know this soupy island, feel more at home with a ball in my hands than I ever have among the tugboats and watermen. Here it's just oysters and crabs and water seeping up through the ground. I want to be on a court that doesn't flood every time the tide comes in. The ocean is a ball hog. Not a team player at all.

It's been done before, leaving this island for the league. Elgin Bolling did it, decades before I was born. Everyone called him Elbow. He had arms like an albatross. Could pluck a ball out of the air and be halfway down the court before the other players could spin on their heels. No one on the mainland ever thinks anyone on our island is worth their salt, but Elbow proved them wrong. Landed a scholarship and left. He wasn't famous, but he made it. Didn't come back until he was doty and getting shorter inch by inch. Just about ready to die.

Elbow was buried in this cemetery on the north end of the island, here by the church that's sliding into the sea, flooded and crawling with marsh critters. I used to go to church in town when I was little, just like everyone else living here still does. But my dad died when I was ten, and after that it was just me and Mom, and she refused to set foot again in a church of any kind. It was after my dad's funeral—the funeral we held without his body, nothing physical for us to say goodbye to—that she lost her faith in this whole unfair world.

We were leaving the church, all our black-clad friends and relations scattering toward their homes in a dissipation of bikes and clusters of people propping each other up as they walked away. "I can't go back, Marty," Mom said to me, taking my hand, pulling me closer to the bulk of her slow-stepping body. Her voice was sad, but unwavering, an echo of every building we walked past. Weather-worn and beaten up by everything the sky could throw at us, but refusing to crumble. But at ten years old, my dad gone and who knew where he was at rest, I saw our little town for what it was: impermanent. Doomed.

"I can't go back," Mom said. "Not until I'm done being mad at God." That made two of us, and I still haven't figured out how to make my peace. Maybe that's what I'm trying to do now, arguing with this storm. Not that I think I'll win, even if I manage not to get knocked down. Somewhere in this furious darkness is everything I've lost, and I'm standing here fighting with the wind and rain, wishing I could change God's bad call.

No one comes up here to the Uppards much anymore. Not since the priest found an old casket floating in the shallows, body still inside with a ring fitted on its bony hand. Seems every day the sea uproots another headstone, takes someone else's relative for its own.

But I always liked coming up the strand to talk with Elbow. His grave was right here, the waterline creeping closer each day like some scavenging dog, ready to grab its prize and drag it away. I'd bring my basketball and sit on it like a little stool next to Elbow, and we'd have conversations. He was helping me with my plan. *Martha*, he'd say. (I kept telling him to call me Marty, like my friends do, but he just wouldn't. Said Martha sounds like a name that's going someplace.) *Martha, are you studying hard? Are you practicing? That's your ticket off this island, Martha. Get yourself a scholarship and go.*

"You don't have to worrysome about that," I'd tell him, flicking the horseflies off his headstone. And then he'd ask to see my whistle, like always, the one I wear around my neck and never take off, not even to shower or sleep. I love the soft, frayed feel of the cord, the small weight of it pert-near my heart. I tuck it into my shirt when I go to school, and I never blow it there, even though there are plenty of reasons why I could. No one likes that Mom and I don't come 'round church on Sundays anymore. And no one understands why I want to wear that black-and-white striped uniform, on the sidelines enforcing a fair game instead of being banged about in the thick of things, where they think I belong.

My dad gave me this whistle when I turned ten. That's how long I've dreamed of being a ref. That birthday was just a week before he drowned, his entire crew caught in a sudden nor'easter that rolled in and dragged their crab boat under and down. A storm not unlike this one, bludgeoning me with all it's got. I still have nightmares about that boat out there at the bottom of the bay, its deadrise rotting among centuries of other wrecks. Keeping company with skipjacks and schooners, freighters and barges and sloops. Abandoned.

When I'm haunted like that, I try to think about my dad's hands, toughened and strong from the sea, when he put the whistle around my neck. The best birthday present I've ever gotten. I hoped to take this whistle all the way to the NBA. "It's right here, Elbow," I'd say, holding it out in my palm like a baby bird. *That's my girl,* he'd tell me, *you hold on to that. It'll keep you strong. It's the onliest thing you need.*

Our school is small, but we still have a girls' basketball team, the Lady Ospreys. Our uniforms are faded and don't match, and none of them fit quite right because they're all hand-me-downs from the boys and the school can't afford to buy us new ones, but we don't care. We don't mind that we're scrappy. That all the mainland teams underestimate us. We're a sneaker wave: they never see us coming, and that's the way we like it.

I'm tall and bulky, so I play center. I love the feeling of posting up against some other big girl, knocking her back a bit and putting one up over her head. My best friend Liz is team captain and point guard. She's short, but she's a solid shot and our team's secret weapon. Our opponents always think she won't be any good because of her height, but then she weaves her way through the defenders, sets up a three, and sails it in. Leaves them all blinking like they've got lighthouses for eyes. Everyone calls her Lizard because she sticks her tongue out, pinned between her lips, when she's concentrating. She does it at the free throw line, but mostly she does it when she's studying, which is practically all the time.

Lizard is wicked smart. When we're not playing basketball, she's doing homework or reading about black holes. She wants to be an astrophysicist. Lizard believes in science, knows it's too late to save our island, though she can't get any of the adults here to listen to her. They're all about erosion and God. But that's not it. It's all the polar ice melting and the ocean rising up to swallow our home. Just look at this nothing of a beach, retreating each year at a rate twice my height, sending bits of pottery and glass, coat buttons and door handles, bodies and their ghosts back out to sea. That's why we've got to go.

Lizard's in on my plan. She helps me stay organized, teaches me how to take good notes, put my thoughts in order for writing, and study for exams. We're going to be seniors when school starts in the fall, and we've been preparing for years. There's not much for kids to do on this island besides hang out and get into trouble, but Lizard keeps me focused, keeps my eye on the ball. She's researched all the colleges, all the scholarships. "Marty," she'll say, looking up from the computer where she's been Googling event horizons and wormholes and college application requirements, "Look at this one. It's got an NCAA team and a scholarship for women in science!"

Most summer afternoons, Lizard and I are out behind the school playing one-on-one, even when the air is hot and humid, buzzing with insects, softening down. The blacktop is cracked and jagged from all the flooding, but we make the best of it. I love the thump-and-ring sound of the ball against the pavement, and the way the chains on the hoop clatter when one of us makes a basket. We like to play HORSE, testing each other's skill, trying out new trick shots. But in my mind, I play another game to keep me thinking about my plan. Each made shot isn't just a letter to me. I'm spelling out possible colleges:

Harvard, Ohio State, Rutgers, Stanford, Eastern Michigan.

Spelling out possible teams: Hornets, Owls, Ramblers, Spartans, Eagles.

Just this morning I was up here at the cemetery, the smell of muck and salty dead things coming off the bay, telling Elbow all about the colleges. I told him about Lizard's and my latest plans. She figures she'll work in a professor's lab. I'll ref kids' games somewhere. We'll be roommates, keep each other on track. Elbow *mmm-hmmed*, told me he knew we would.

Mom's too busy keeping us afloat to believe in me and my plans. Other than shedding crab for their husbands, there aren't a lot of jobs for women here, so my mom works showing tourists around our island, driving them in a golf cart down the narrow streets. They come to see how we're disappearing, take pictures of the half-sunken buildings, street signs and crosses poking up out of the marshes as osprey fly over the bay. The tourists look at us funny for the way we talk backwards or for our old-fashioned accents, our brogue-ish vowels stretched out loud and long. They shake their heads like they can't believe we're still living here, then leave.

It's like over and back, Martha, Elbow told me. His use of basketball as an analogy for life is one reason we got along so well.

Those tourists, he said, *they're just come-heres on our side of the water, like crossing the half court line. But the island's not theirs, they're not really touching it, and so they can just go right back home. Ain't nobody going to stop them.*

I sat on my basketball and listened, polished up my whistle by rubbing it between my finger and thumb, buffing the silver to a perfect gleam. *But us,* he said, *not so easy. When we leave this place, we try to carry it with us, to keep possession of it, but we can't really. We have to make the turnover. Can't have it both ways. Once you leave, you can't go home again.*

"But you came back, Elbow," I argued. I rested my arm on his stone, which was leaning a little more than usual, tilting toward the bay. He was quiet a minute, thinking it over like he always did. *That's a whole-nother thing,* he said. *I was just a whiff of myself, nearly done.* Elbow was always going on about leaving the island. I knew he wanted me to go out there in the world, but I think part of him wished I would stay, maybe thought I wouldn't ever come back. There's not a lot of us from-heres left.

I had the whistle good and shiny. "Listen to this, Elbow," I said. I put the whistle to my lips and gave it a good long blow. A little warble that became a full, shrill scream. Birds flew up like snapjacks at the sound, fireworks of feathers in all directions. Two cats sprinted out of the empty church like they'd got devils on their tails, and Elbow and I had a good laugh about it. But just then the clouds doubled up, as if I'd called them in with my racket. The wind pushed the water toward shore, and I gave the air a cautious sniff, thinking this hurricane the weather folks had been talking about all week might make landfall after all. I should have known this monster of a storm swamping and walloping me now was on the way.

"I've gotta go," I told Elbow. "Lizard and I are going to wait out this storm together tonight, work on college essays." I shouldered my backpack, picked up my ball and did a little dribble on top of his grave for him. High fived his slouching headstone with my palm. I wish I'd known I wasn't going to get the chance at a proper goodbye.

When I got to Lizard's house, the tide was in, and I had to wade through the water to get to her doorstep. This happens all the time, but the flooding was even deeper than usual with the storm rolling in. I took off my sneakers and socks and held them over my head with one hand, my ball in the other, but I still ended up sopped and hucky. Lizard was waiting for me at the door with a towel over her arm, laughing.

"'Ell, you're early," she scolded—that's backwards talk, meaning I was late. We islanders put 'ell at the beginning of all sorts of things to turn them 'round to the opposite of what they'd usually mean, a habit we have to tone down for the tourists. My mom practices her tour guide scripts so she doesn't slip up and confuse folks. "You look like you've been out mudlarking or something," Lizard teased. We used to do that together as kids: run free through the marshes, wade in the shallows looking for treasures and crabs. "Come from the Uppards again?"

Lizard knows I like to visit this little church, that I find some sort of comfort up here, but she doesn't really know why. She's my best friend, but I don't know what she'd think about me talking to ghosts. Especially one that's not even my dad. I took the towel and dried off my big feet. "Yeah," I said, and slung my backpack onto a nearby chair. I was set to sleep over, ride out this storm. Lizard said we should get right down to it. We had a long night ahead of us writing essays and listening to the rain pound the island, turn it mostly to briny sea.

The essay I've been working on, like my game, is not just about the letters:

H: How to write about beating the odds and not sound like a cornball.

O: Over and back, that's what it's about. Figuring out how to leave home.

R: Referee. How life is about the rules, and making something fair and beautiful out of that.

S: Sinking. I know about metaphors. How to use the island as one.

E: Elevate. Like my tall body soaring toward the basket. Like the Lady Ospreys winning last year's regional tourney when no one thought we could. Like even though this island is both a hook and a stone in my chest, I'm trying to get myself above the surface.

Lizard's essay is about growing up on the island, trying to be an astrophysicist, when practically everyone we know is telling her that a girl can't be a scientist and also that science is just plain wrong. Because erosion and God, like I said. And how erosion and God are big and powerful and true, but that doesn't mean they have any sway over the icebergs melting and raising up the ocean over our island, taking all our dreams down with it. When I think about Lizard's essay, I think about the stars looking down at us, already dead way out there light years away, like they're waving goodbye because they know how all this is going to end. But if anyone can fight back, it's Lizard. Typing a mile a minute, her tongue sticking out between her lips, she's up for it.

We'd been hunkered down writing for hours when Lizard suddenly stopped typing. "Hey Marty," she said. "Listen to that."

The rain was really coming down. Buckets, sheets, cats and dogs, all of it. Big winds clobbering the walls of the house. Water sloshed at Lizard's front steps, like it was knocking to come in. We've weathered our share of hurricanes living here, but I should have known this one was different. Determined. There are storms, and then there are *storms*. I pictured my mom up listening to the wind and rain, wondering if tomorrow there would be anything left for the tourists to see. The last big hurricane took out a bunch of our crab shanties—the way so many folks here make their living—and not one of them got rebuilt. What will happen to my mom, to our island, if I leave? I thought about this little sinking church, about the cats and devils likely making for the rafters. And Elbow. Elbow and his lopsided grave.

I pulled on my shoes and made for the door. Lizard knew what I was thinking, like she always does. She looked me right in the eyes, snapped into point guard mode, team captain mode. "Marty," she said, calm and urgent. "You need to sit this one out. It's too dangerous. You can check on the church in the morning." She stood and put her hands on my arms like she was breaking up a fight on the court, trying to get me to back down.

It wasn't just about the church, but I couldn't explain that just then. I wasn't sure she'd understand, and I didn't have time to convince her. "I need to know now," I protested, working to shake off her grip.

"Marty, what do you think you're going to do? You can't keep the ocean from coming. That's just the way it is."

I knew she was right, but that didn't hold back my sad muscle of a heart. "Lizard, I have to," I said, twisting away from her. "Let me go." How could I explain what Elbow meant to me, someone to talk to when I couldn't visit my dad, out there just bones at the bottom of the bay? I wanted to call the shots this time, call foul on this world taking all I had left from me.

Before she could block me, I was out the front door into the airish darkness. I splashed through the rising water shoes and all, running like it was the last few seconds of a game where we're down by one, and everything depends on how this next play goes. I was holding my breath and panting all at the same time, making for the Uppards through the downpour, my big body pushing against the wind, pushing debris out of my way. Bits of our town flying and floating all around me—everything that wasn't boarded up or battened down. I could hear Lizard's voice behind me, calling me to come back, and I hoped like crazy she wouldn't try to follow. These winds would pick her up and carry her across the bay. So I did the only thing I could think to keep me focused:

H: Hold on, Elbow, hold on.

O: Ocean, don't take my friend away.

R: Run. Run, run, run.

S: Stay. Please, please stay.

E: Elbow. Elbow, don't leave me.

I sprinted through churning pools of water like I was on some sort of wild fast break when it hit me, the thought of my dad's boat out in the storm. How gales like these must have spun his craft around like it carried no weight at all. How the winds would have plucked piles of blue crabs from the hull, tossed them clacking and flailing into the swells. How my dad would have reached his big fisherman arms up through the waves, trying to push the whole raging ocean down to swim back to me.

I struggled my way up the shoreline, the church just in sight ahead of me, and already I knew. What was left of the church was leaning, its skeleton of beams lifting up out of the ground, starting to topple. I picked up speed, wiping the rain from my face, trying to see this ruin of a cemetery with its litter of stones. "Elbow!" I called out, "Elbow, are you there?"

I reached the waterline, this new waterline, and my feet sank into the mud. Elbow's headstone was gone, washed away, not even a hole where it used to be. I strained to see out into the bay, but it was all dark clouds and whitecaps. No headstone. No Elbow. The loss hit me harder than the wind. Just like when my dad died, out there in the angry sea. Final.

And just like that, I wasn't sure about my plan anymore. I know if I leave, I may not have the choice to come back. There might not be an island left to come home to. I hold my whistle tightly inside my fist.

The wind is howling something fierce, trying to knock me down. I stand at the new edge of the island, where Elbow's grave isn't anymore. It does no good to be mad at the weather, at the ocean and its humans-be-damned greed. But I raise up my whistle anyway. Put it to my lips as the storm slaps my face to remind me I'm smaller than I think. I don't care. I blow with all my might, the whistle a sharp howl against the squall. I hope Elbow can hear me. That my dad can hear me. And the ocean, and the icebergs, and the stars. I stand my ground, what's left of it. And I blow and blow and blow.

The Auction House

The Auction House has no address. It's never in one place for more than a few hours before it moves on, like a traveling circus or a flock of migrating birds. Though there are no advertisements or social media campaigns, the patrons know how to find it, when to arrive, and what's at stake. The Auction House could manifest anywhere—a barn, a mausoleum, a forgotten underground tunnel—depending on the item up for sale. Only a single item is on offer each time The Auction House assembles itself and opens its doors. Always an item indicative of the tug-of-war between the human species and nature's violent indifference.

Inside her chest, Zofia's heart is a hummingbird, beating so quickly she feels it might blur her invisible. Her presence here tonight is the culmination of several months of work. The Auction House is the subject of Zofia's doctoral dissertation. Since the mass extinction began, universities have given up their sprawling, manicured lawns. Their historic buildings are no longer well preserved. Natural resources are too precious to waste on aesthetics. The tar pit of collective despair drags most ambitions down, and the pursuit of higher education on a dying planet is left to the stubbornly optimistic few. Those who make it as far as Zofia are a clever and resourceful lot. Their elaborately architected studies are a series of stouthearted attempts to either document or attempt to reverse The Damage That's Been Done.

On this sweltering midsummer evening, The Auction House is ensconced inside an abandoned airplane hangar. A few dozen patrons are beginning to gather outside, impatient for the moment they'll be let in. Zofia is glad for the change of scenery. Her little apartment near the university looks out onto a street lined with blackened trees that have crumpled from the smog. People spend little time outdoors, and the birds and rodents have fled, though Zofia can't imagine where to. She traveled for days to reach the site of the hangar, which, though treeless, is also free of the piles of garbage and debris that are commonplace in every urban district.

Zofia wanders through the few dozen people, collecting snippets of speculative conversation as if netting butterflies. The oppressive heat, which everyone has become accustomed to in recent years, does little to squelch the eager patrons—the anticipation of what's to come seemingly as enjoyable as the event itself.

Zofia threads her way to the rim of the crowd and watches the patrons accumulate, waiting for the arrival of two particular individuals: The Zoologist and The Collector. The auctiongoers' outfits appear meticulously coordinated, designed to encapsulate the identity of each patron with singular effect. Zofia marvels at their ingenuity—how they have fashioned elaborate apparel from materials at hand. A dress constructed from caution tape and bits of silk. A vest woven entirely of electrical charging cords. In a world where reuse is paramount, only the most creative individuals have managed to thrive.

Zofia's mother taught her to sew at a young age, a skill that she is now very glad to have. She has tailored her own attire for the occasion, and her outfit, like her dissertation, is focused on the extraordinary nature of The Auction House's wares. Zofia has assembled her dress from scraps of animal-print fabric, giraffe spots and the markings of a multitude of patterned cats converging improbably to flatter her slim form. As the dress descends, the prints lessen, fading to the emptiness of black at the flaring hem. At the zebra-striped v-line of her neck, a thimble dangles from a chain. The thimble is all Zofia has left of her parents, of her home, leveled in one of the great hurricanes that signaled the beginning of the mass extinction. The thimble is always prominently visible. Zofia's abundant, fiery hair, however, is tonight in a tight bun hidden beneath a Victorian-styled feather array.

Zofia's heart steadies as she notices a familiar face arrowing toward her through the crowd. Though she has fiercely studied its two most prominent patrons, The Auction House is not something one finds on one's own.

Ferris attends the same university as Zofia, and he is taken with her in a bothersome, unguarded way. On a planet in turmoil, where everyone must regularly navigate natural disasters, falling in love is one of the few remaining salves. Zofia, however, regards romance as futile until someone figures out What Should Be Done. She feels affection for Ferris, but she is determined not to get too enamored of anyone.

When Zofia started researching her thesis, she focused equally on tracking The Zoologist and The Collector. Since the mass extinction began, the two have been in an unspoken competition, at opposite ends of the spectrum of What Should Be Done. This rivalry is the reason Zofia is at The Auction House tonight. Zofia has followed The Zoologist down every rabbit hole. But The Collector is especially elusive. Until she met Ferris, The Collector and The Auction House were both nearly impossible to pursue.

"I knew you'd find it," Ferris praises her. His perpetually winsome face is buoyed with excitement. Each patron must independently discover The Auction House's location by solving a scavenger-hunt style invitation from a current patron. Zofia is pleased that her extensive sleuthing and navigation of Ferris's cryptic clues have paid off, though she bristles at the flattery. "I've been looking for you since I arrived."

Ferris's clothing reflects his own field of study: devising a low-energy solution for desalinating seawater. His suit is a brilliant blue, rumpled and glossy, with little salt shakers peeking from every pocket. He's crowned by a top hat decorated with tubes and filter parts from failed attempts in the lab. Ferris wears his disarray proudly, his tousled features somehow charming, his wrinkled attire whimsically formal. His outward manner is so affable one would never suspect that his mother had wasted away from cancer, or that his father barely acknowledges that he exists.

Zofia lays her hand on Ferris's arm for just a moment. "I'm trying to blend in."

Ferris leans closer to her. "A masterful bit of dressmaking, and quite the statement about extinction, but it's hardly camouflage. You look amazing."

Zofia flushes beneath her multiple animal skins. She takes a small step back, fingering the thimble and wishing for a breeze. "Do you think it will be any cooler inside?"

"I somehow doubt it." Ferris's eyes are gently amused. "Any questions before it begins?"

Much of what Zofia has learned about The Auction House has come from Ferris, which is the main reason she indulges his fondness for her. Opportunely, he is The Collector's son, though he has not shared this information with anyone but Zofia. Such is his disdain for his father's preoccupation. Zofia knows that once they are welcomed in, they will be forbidden to speak to one another. The Auction House is a silent affair except for the rapid cantillating of the Auctioneer.

Zofia is well prepared. She feels like she did as a child, reading the same story over and over again, but suddenly the characters from the page are real. "I'm ready," she says, "to finally see things for myself." Zofia has rehearsed this moment in her mind throughout all the time she's been searching for The Auction House.

Zofia knows The Auctioneer will be wearing a wig with bangs that fall in front of her eyes, covering the top half of her face. Her gown will be patterned to match the item to be sold. No one—not Ferris with his connections nor Zofia after her extensive research—knows who The Auctioneer is or where she goes after The

Auction House closes its doors and vanishes, collapsing like a dying star.

The patrons are growing restless as the sun inches mercifully lower, their voices and bodies murmurating as they shift about the hangar, waiting for The Auction House to open its doors. As Zofia directs a stray feather away from her eyes, Ferris motions toward the hazy sky. "Look," he says. An ironic smile pulls at the corners of his mouth. "My father is arriving."

A hot air balloon emerges as if uncloaked. This is one of the moments Zofia has been waiting for, and she allows Ferris to loop his arm through hers. The balloon is the color of the sky, which is tinted grayish orange from the perpetual wildfires and volcanic eruptions that burden the weather-beaten planet. This makes the balloon difficult to keep track of for more than a few moments.

As the mass extinction has drawn on, fossil fuels have become scarce. Motor vehicles have fallen out of use, burying entire landscapes under piles of chassis and metal hulls that have become their own kind of mountain ranges. Airplanes, too, are grounded, the little international travel that does happen reverting back to ships. The Collector is one of the few with the means to maintain his own hot air balloon, and it is the only way he travels.

As Zofia and Ferris look on, the patrons spread apart so the balloon can land. The Collector dismounts from the basket and tethers it carefully in place at the hangar's edge. Zofia sees the family resemblance immediately, though The Collector is clearly the tidier version of his son. She is about to plead with Ferris to introduce her to his father, but a sudden hush has fallen over the patrons. The doors of the airplane hangar have begun to lift.

After a dramatic bout of hydraulic creaking, Zofia can make out the silhouette of a ship—the kind whose renderings she has only seen in history books. A ghost of a ship, from a time when the oceans were still mysterious and blue. Ferris leans into Zofia, pointing, and silently draws her attention to a space below the figurehead. In front of the ship stands The Auctioneer.

The Auctioneer has the appearance of being oft-assembled. As if she's been folded up, limb over slender limb, creased and soft like a photograph carried in a beloved's breast pocket long after the beloved's beloved has passed away. The bottom half of her face, visible below the fall of dark bangs, is pulled into a curious grin. She wears a long cloak, masking the gown Zofia knows must be hidden beneath.

In her bird-trilling voice, The Auctioneer explains that tonight's venue is a Dutch vessel that has remarkably survived since the sixteenth century, safekept in the hangar by a benefactor of considerable wealth. The decayed front of the ship forms a natural doorway, and the patrons are to be seated within the skeletal hull.

The Auctioneer invites them in, and Zofia hangs back, wanting to be the last to enter. Ferris hasn't left her side, and Zofia finds she doesn't mind. She inclines her head toward him, accepting his company as they follow the crowd in.

The rows of chairs are nearly full, the expectation in the silent crowd like an egg balanced at the end of a spoon. Zofia and Ferris sit off to one side in a naturally elevated indentation in the vessel's curving hull, where they have a good view of the patrons.

And there, in the front row, is the second individual Zofia's been waiting to see. Positioned across from The Auctioneer, The Zoologist is like a funhouse reflection, everything about her a bit askew. She bounces one leg in a small, rapid tremble but is otherwise perfectly still, her auction paddle balanced across her lap. She is muddied and uncostumed, ostensibly having come directly from her fieldwork, and is accompanied by some manner of insects scuttling in a jar at her feet.

Ferris's father has taken the seat next to The Zoologist. His legs and arms are crossed over one another, neat as laminated pastry in the folds of his shimmering suit. He stares straight ahead at The Auctioneer, paddle at the ready, oblivious to the presence of his son some distance behind him. The Collector occasionally glances down at The Zoologist's captives, perhaps hoping to be surprised by something he hasn't seen for years. The Zoologist seems unperturbed by the proximity of The Collector, though she toes the jar more securely between her feet.

Zofia opens a notebook. No electronics are allowed inside The Auction House. No cell phones, no cameras, no recording devices of any kind. This gives The Auction House a temporal suspension, creates a welcome diversion in a world hurtling toward nonexistence. Most of tonight's patrons don't have the means to bid. They've come for the show.

The item on offer at the Auction House is always a matter of much curiosity. The Auctioneer will draw out the suspense as long as possible, letting the patrons size her up, divining clues about the item from her gown. She'll tease them, rotating slowly so they can see all aspects of the puzzle, though the auction items are so unusual that rarely does anyone guess correctly. Zofia has made record of them all.

At the last auction, held in one of Ireland's few remaining forests, the object for sale was a round of wood, the cross section of a tree from 536 A.D. Before the mass extinction, historians generally agreed that 536 was the worst year to have been alive on Earth. That year, a series of massive volcanic eruptions plunged the world into darkness, bringing bitter cold, famine, and plague that would last for 18 months. It was by studying the rings of these ancient trees, drastically altered in their growth during the period when ash blocked out the sun, that scientists were able to account for what had happened. On the night of that auction, The Auctioneer wore a gown of cadaverous charcoal, whorled with rings to suggest the growth of a tree, her skin unaccountably bluish and sallow.

Since she was a young girl, Zofia has been enraptured with The Zoologist. She has read every article The Zoologist has ever published, has pored over the results of all of her studies, meditating on the data as if it were a rosary, each number a glassy bead she worries in the palm of her mind. In the wake of the mass extinction, The Zoologist has become a sort of traveling hermit, moving from country to country to study and document the planet's decline, shutting herself up into field stations and labs as she looks for the answers to What Should Be Done.

The Zoologist is a being of juxtaposition. On the one hand is her existential gloom, the knowledge that her years of warnings, pleadings to The Decision Makers about the tumults of the world's climate, went unheeded. The realization that she and all the other scientists were soothsayers with accumulating lava flows of evidence at their backs, and still they failed to prevent The Damage That's Been Done. On the other hand is The Zoologist's ontological certainty, her unflappable optimism that she can somehow resurrect What Has Been Lost.

Tonight, The Zoologist appears anxious, her disquiet evident in the quaver of her leg. Zofia guesses that the jar at The Zoologist's feet contains bush-crickets, some of the last of their kind. The Collector eyes them hungrily. Zofia watches The Zoologist with longing, hardly believing she is looking upon her at last, but she knows she cannot speak with her yet. After all, The Auction House is a silent affair.

Zofia has devoted an entire chapter of her dissertation to the only time a patron made the mistake of making a sound at an auction. That evening, the item was an annotated copy of *On the Origin of Species*, a complete bound set of manuscript sheets overgrown with Darwin's handwritten revisions for his German translator. The Auctioneer was festooned in a gown constructed entirely of book pages, scalloped in an intricate filigree of folds in which nested several finches fashioned from tissue paper and parchment feathers. As The Auctioneer spun, the paper birds appeared to be feeding on the words that blurred in an inky swirl. The patron failed to contain his excitement when *Species* was unveiled, crying out as he raised his paddle, and The Auction House nearly shattered with the sound. All light in the room was immediately snuffed, and when it was relit, the patron had vanished. The Auction House carries with it an understanding. No questions were ever asked.

As they wait, Zofia watches Ferris's face roil between shame and yearning as he stares at his father. Zofia's original hypothesis, which Ferris has confirmed, was that The Collector intends to be the last person on Earth—a disturbing ambition given his paternal state. He aims to surround himself with one specimen from every creature that ever existed. The Collector will be the last human, the final piece in his collection, to be found by whatever intelligent species inhabits the planet next. The Auction House is a reliable source of specimens for The Collector's project, to which he has devoted himself since his wife's death. Ferris has told Zofia, not without some measure of sadness and humiliation, about his father's growing hoard: a black rhino horn, baleen bristles of a blue whale, a pelt of one of the last polar bears to roam the remaining slivers of arctic ice.

Zofia is fascinated by how The Zoologist and The Collector's disparate projects set them at odds. They want to obtain the same things, for very different reasons. The Zoologist is extracting DNA from the specimens she purchases and captures, cataloging it in the hopes of someday bringing all the plants and animals back. This goal is explicit in The Zoologist's abundant journal articles and is the impetus for those who fund her excursions, her research, and her visits to The Auction House to procure the rare remains of What Has Been Lost. The Collector, however, has accepted the mass extinction as inevitable and is looking to use the wealth he amassed by contributing to The Damage That's Been Done to secure his place in a complete accounting that no humans will be left to appreciate.

While Zofia studies The Zoologist and The Collector, she rolls the thimble back and forth between her finger and thumb, waiting. With his shoulder lightly pressed against Zofia's, Ferris has now trained all his attention on The Auctioneer, who is standing stock-still on the stage, eyes closed. Zofia finds it unsettling that The Collector, who must know that Ferris is here, remains so indifferent to his son. To distract herself, Zofia plays a guessing game inside her head about what the item on offer tonight will be. She begins with the venue, sure to be well suited to the prize. She wracks her brain for anything she might have studied about merchant ships but comes up with nothing. Zofia can hear the ancient boards whisper their little knocks and creaks all around her, can feel the looming presence of the towering masts.

And then comes the moment Zofia has been waiting for years to witness. The Auctioneer flashes her cat-like grin, drops her cloak to the floor of the stage. Her skin is milky white, and she glows like an apparition in the bow of the ship. She extends her arms and begins a slow spin, flaunting her clue of a gown. Quickly, Zofia begins to sketch, like a naturalist recording an animal in its habitat, wanting to get every detail of this evening exactly right.

Tonight The Auctioneer is wearing a sari, unusually styled entirely in black. Around her neck dangles a nineteenth century pocket watch. As The Auctioneer turns, the watch sways hypnotically, and a small series of puddles appears and spirals around her on the floor. Zofia realizes with surprise that the sari fits so snugly because it is soaking wet. As The Auctioneer continues to spin and walk an uneven pattern about the stage, she produces a little box. When she opens it, Zofia and the patrons all lean closer to see its contents: a collection of confections that The Auctioneer begins to distribute as she walks through the crowd, offering a sweet to each person.

Zofia is jolted to a memory from childhood—her parents reading to her each evening before bedtime, all three of them tucked close together on the overstuffed couch. She leaves off her sketching and, clutching the thimble around her neck, feels the uncanniness of the coincidence. She is suddenly certain what the item on offer will be. Ferris doesn't seem to be working through the puzzle at all but is instead licking the last bits of sugar from his fingertips as The Auctioneer moves from him to Zofia. The Auctioneer's eyes are obscured by her sheet of bangs, but Zofia can feel the depth of her stare as she holds out her now empty box, nothing left in it to offer.

It's as if Zofia has fallen into the pages of *Alice in Wonderland*. This is, she realizes, a reenactment of the Caucus-race, when Alice and several other creatures must run about haphazardly to dry themselves off after swimming in a pool of Alice's tears. Confections are given as prizes to all but Alice, who is left with only the thimble she already had in her pocket. The Auctioneer is still standing before Zofia, who holds tight to her own thimble, reeling with the knowledge of what is to come. Zofia knows who orchestrated the Caucus-race. It was the Dodo.

Everyone, including The Zoologist and The Collector, has turned to see why The Auctioneer has stalled. Zofia feels she might dematerialize from the rapid beating of her heart, so she meets The Zoologist's gaze. The Zoologist's eyes are worried, and Zofia holds them within her own, knowing this may be her only moment of connection. Then Zofia notices The Collector regarding her as if she is some new kind of beast, no doubt trying to work out who is sitting next to his son. But The Auctioneer only smiles wider, somehow satisfied. She spins abruptly and heads back to the stage. It's time for the auction to begin.

From the spectral planks of the ship, The Auctioneer brings forth the item. Just as Zofia predicted, before her are the remains of a dodo bird. In the sixteenth century, Dutch sailors discovered the dodo on the island of Mauritius and helped push the fowl toward extinction in less than a century. The dodo is larger than Zofia would have thought, just over two feet tall, and constructed entirely of bones. The most famous of all extinct species, the dodo is the original harbinger of What Has Been Lost. Both The Zoologist and The Collector sit up straighter, grip their paddles in anticipation.

As The Auctioneer's lilting voice describes the bird, Zofia scribbles furiously. The composite skeleton, the only existing remnants of the species, was assembled from a smattering of bones unearthed from the Mauritian swamp Mare au Songes in the 1860s and pieced together by an amateur scientist, two hundred years after the bird went extinct. It's the same period during which Lewis Carroll was inventing Alice's adventures and Darwin's *Origin of Species* was bringing the importance of extinction to light. Zofia feels the clues coming together, the enormity of their accordance. Nothing in The Auction House ever happens by accident.

Zofia understands what The Zoologist would give for this specimen, to practice de-extinction on the species that awakened humans to their impact on the natural world. What The Collector wouldn't do for this mishmash of bones, a Holy Grail of an animal to place beside him at The End of the World. Zofia pauses over her notebook, inhales the electricity of the audience. What Should Be Done pulses through the splintered ship. And the bidding begins.

Before long, as nearly every auction goes, The Zoologist and The Collector are the only bidders still raising their paddles, back and forth in a maddening exchange. The Auctioneer's voice is the warble of a songbird and the rattle of a crow all at once, filling the silent ship and echoing into the hangar beyond. The patrons are balanced like fledglings at the edges of their seats. Zofia wonders who Ferris is rooting for—his father, out of some misplaced loyalty, or The Zoologist, who would see everyone saved. She squeezes his hand, claiming him for her side, and he turns with surprise, beaming in his cerulean suit. The bidding goes on for so long that The Auctioneer's sari completely dries. The Zoologist looks more nervous than ever as The Collector smugly squares his shoulders, calmly lifts his paddle again. With growing dismay, Zofia senses that The Zoologist is going to be outbid.

Zofia chose sides long ago. Of course she wants The Zoologist to win. She wants the same thing The Zoologist wants. For the relentless smoke and rising water of their world to settle. For the sky to come back to blue. To be able to breathe again, to be able to wander through a forest, for all of the animals to return. Who could abide The Collector and his selfish project, all the world's varied beauty catalogued and locked away?

Zofia turns her eyes to meet Ferris's, silently pleading for his help. But what can he do, a son outcast by his father, not worthy of being collected? The Auctioneer is calling out over the crowded, silent room: *Going once.* The Zoologist has dropped her windblown nest of a head in resignation. *Going twice.* If Something Must Be Done, it will have to be done by Zofia herself.

Zofia grasps at the thimble around her neck, yanks the chain free and holds it in her palm. It's just a trinket, nothing more than a reminder of when she was a girl, when the world was just teetering, before the mass extinction began. Zofia unfolds her fist, places the thimble on her index finger, stands and raises her hand into the air. She shouts into the speechless hull of the ship.

"Stop!"

In unison, the patrons inhale a silent gasp. The Auctioneer halts before the word *Gone* can fall from her lips. The Zoologist and The Collector swivel to face Zofia, their paddles falling still at their sides. Ferris is pulling at the animal folds of Zofia's dress, trying to get her to sit down, but it's too late. Everyone takes stock of the thimble being offered as trade. Zofia isn't sure what will come next, or what consequences will follow, but she knows she cannot leave unless the dodo is delivered into The Zoologist's hands. It is most assuredly What Should Be Done.

The thimble sparkles at the tip of Zofia's finger, and The Auctioneer smiles her wide smile. The Auction House carries with it an understanding. The lights go out.

A greater silence descends upon the ship. Somewhere in the pitch black are the masts, and the crow's nest, and the rudder. Zofia breathes in, summoning the smell of the sea, but inhales instead the salty-sweet odor of Ferris's watery suit, feels his arm protectively circle her waist. Before Zofia can move a muscle, The Auctioneer's wig brushes against her neck and she purls into Zofia's ear: *Time to stitch up the world.* Zofia feels the thimble being lifted from her finger, its loss a small, heavy ache in her chest. She accepts into her arms the weight of centuries of bones, flightless and wandering into the hole opening up in her heart.

Zofia imagines The Zoologist and The Collector in the darkness, both of them contemplating What Has Been Lost. There is little time. She closes her arms gently around the conglomerate of bones, leans her face into the bulbous beak.

Zofia reaches for Ferris, her fluttering heart tipping its way toward his. She pulls him close, brushes her lips swiftly across his cheek to whisper in his ear, "Do this for me, Ferris. Bring the Zoologist to your father's balloon. Quickly!" The Collector's son does as he is asked.

Zofia navigates her way through the dark, cradling the dodo as she stumbles toward the opening in the ship. She must find her way to the edge of the hangar before the lights of The Auction House come back up. She reaches the balloon, her heart beating so fast she feels she might lift off the ground on her own, and carefully climbs into the basket with the dodo balanced against her chest. Ferris and

The Zoologist are close behind her, Ferris already bending to unanchor the craft.

The patrons are now rushing from the hangar, finding their voices in the stifling midsummer gloom. From the rising wicker basket, Zofia and The Zoologist watch as The Collector strides through the chattering crowd to discover his balloon has been unmoored. He shouts up at his son, the careful folds of his suit now flapping around him as if he's drowning, a forgotten creature against the shadow of the ship.

Ferris does not look down as he steers the balloon and its passengers into the refuge of the sky, seemingly unbothered by his betrayal. The Zoologist holds the dodo in a kind of reverent trance. Zofia can feel that something has shifted. In breaking the rules, The Auctioneer has taken sides, as well. Zofia is certain that wherever The Auctioneer may disappear to, The Auction House will likewise vanish. That this evening will be its last. The Auctioneer taps her pocket watch, fades back into the bilge of the ship. As the balloon ascends, Zofia touches the space at her neckline, fingers tracing the empty line of her collarbone. The Auction House shudders. The hangar folds in on itself, closing its doors and ushering the patrons back into the clamorous night.

The Torture Orchard

I came to work in this orchard for the trees. You'd think I might have been driven by a desire to help my own kind—the future humans whose food supply is balanced precariously on the edge of every ray of sun—but no. This place is a kind of underworld above ground, all suffering on display. I carry out my tasks: withhold water, measure the extent of stress, taste the ripened or unripened fruit. But what no one knows is that, as I walk the acres of dry ground, rows and rows of tormented beings, I feel their diminishment in my bones. As my own body wanes, I try to comfort the trees. Apologize for their pain.

In the torture orchard, many of the trees are drupes, stone fruits with a seed shelled inside sweet flesh. Peaches, plums, apricots, olives. And almonds, their pink and white blossoms abundant in the rising heat. What if we could breed an almond tree that didn't require gallons of water pumped from dwindling stores underground? The almonds here must grow on nothing but what falls from the sky, or doesn't. The failures crackle and blacken, are plucked away. The ones that thrive offer their slender kernels to our calculating hands.

The experiment began with the pistachio trees. We assumed they would languish, growing in soil so salty and parched. But every one of them survived the summer. We didn't understand then about the long-term effects. How a thirst like that would change them. You know how when a bitch is malnourished, the pups may all be whelped alive but they will be sickly, runtish? It was like that. Seasons later, the nuts were tiny, nothing you would want to eat.

Each year, the land here grows drier and drier. Drought plagues the earth, and wildfires lick hungrily at our doorstep. The rows of this orchard are lined with dust, sometimes with ash. The trees die, or they endure. In their meager shade, we bend over our scientific instruments, squint at gauges as needles stutter and rise. We measure water tension in the trees. When the tension is high, the trees are struggling to suction moisture from the soil. Water in the bodies of trees is like blood in our veins. As the pressure rises, the body falters.

Though you wouldn't guess it from our cruelty to this orchard, the pistachio has long been revered. They are said to have grown in the Garden of Eden. Nebuchadnezzar, king of Babylon, planted them in his fabled hanging gardens. The Queen of Sheba deemed pistachios the food of royalty. I think of crowns of trees, branches of government, roots that determine the life you're allowed to live. The land that raised me shaped how I grew into the world. I carry it like an invisible sheath on my skin.

On the farm where I grew up, the animals sorted themselves. Baby goats played king of the mountain, knocking at each other with buttoned horns. The biggest chickens bullied their way to the top of the flock. Even the dogs knew who must turn belly up and who was allowed to stare. As a child, I should have been plump on goat's milk, cured bacon, fresh eggs. Should have been strong from the work. Even my name, Sharon—*fertile plain*—promises abundance. But I was neither vigorous nor stout. Thin as a dousing stick, I was pulled one way or another by my parents' dreams and demands.

When I was little, I wished to disappear, like the naiad Daphne, into a tree. My two younger brothers both thought themselves gods, or the sun. Blazing eyes at the center of the world. Anything around which lesser beings revolved. They resented the work of the farm: all its bestial needs, the insistence of the soil. In their mouths, my name sounded muddy and spoiled. *Scrawny Sharon,*

Skeleton Sharon. They gnawed at me while I scattered chicken feed and gathered eggs. They would chase me to the edge of the horse pasture, knock me down in the dirt. *Please turn me into a tree,* I begged the ground beneath me as the horses shied away from my brothers' rough jeers. But I was a little silverfish curled in the fescue, no one's to save.

And so I buried myself in books, stories of gods and goddesses whose troubles I might compare to my own. Of all the myths I read as a child, I loved Persephone best. As I weeded my mother's garden, I imagined Persephone gathering flowers in a meadow. How the ground cracked open and Hades appeared in his horse-drawn chariot, dragged her down to the underworld, and made her his bride. It was the consumption of six pomegranate seeds that bound Persephone to the realm of the dead. Some say Persephone was tricked by Hades, who appealed to her rankling hunger and offered the fruit. Others say she chose willingly, deliberately placed each seed in her mouth and swallowed them down.

There are pomegranates in the torture orchard, too. If these trees could grow in the underworld, among the dead and their king, then surely they can survive our cruel withholdings. These human-made trials are nothing compared to the patience and endurance of a tree. Every season, they defy our attempts to cripple them.

Persephone's mother, Demeter, goddess of agriculture and the harvest, was devastated by the loss of her daughter. I often wonder if my mother was as attached to me. Her affections were sparse, her demeanor toward me cold. Was it only my compliance, my care for the farm, that made her love me? Demeter struck a bargain to return her daughter aboveground for two-thirds of every year. Thus Persephone became a dual goddess, of both fertility and death. It's Persephone I think of when I walk the long rows of this orchard, the trees negotiating between fecundity and famine, my own body an echo of their spindly forms.

"Sharon!"

My name on the dry wind from the end of a row of persimmons. Sometimes I think I hear my name coming from the trees themselves. But the alligator-bark of the persimmons is silent, simply enduring the stifling temperature of the August afternoon. I straighten unsteadily from where I'm crouched at the base of a rugged tree trunk, sampling the soil. My clothes hang loosely on my body, all the same hue as the dusty ground. My hair is twisted in two long braids beneath a ball cap, my head too warm, damp with sweat. I squint down the aisle of orbless trees.

"Sharon! Over here!"

It's Mateo, standing at the end of the row with a pump-up pressure chamber tucked under his arm. His face is soft brown, like walnut bark, his smile a crease of light. He cradles the rectangular metal box in one hand, a long pole extending downward from its base. Pressed to his hip, it looks like a sword. Or a pogo stick on its side. Either suits Mateo equally. He and I were grad students together, graduated this past spring. We were both drawn to the research happening in this experimental orchard managed by the university.

"Mateo!" I raise my arm in a wave, then brush the dirt off my hands against my shirt. My belly is caving in again; I can feel the bony rise of my ribs. The dizziness comes and goes, especially on these sweltering afternoons, and I close my eyes, then slowly open them. As Mateo makes his way toward me, I hook my thumbs in the pockets of my linen pants, try to make myself appear as formidable as the tree I stand beside, hoping Mateo won't notice my tremor and sway.

"Hey, Shar." My name is warm when he says it, nothing like how it sounds in the voices of my brothers. Even as adults, I can still hear the disdain in their voices. Though drought racks our farm, my brothers will never believe that the end of our human existence stalks so closely.

Mateo has always been kind to me, has never made me feel like a slighted thing. We liked each other the moment we met, talked for hours over coffee after our first day of class. Agricultural sciences, horticulture, environmental law—we studied together, took care of one another, pulled each other through.

"Do you have time to help me with the almonds, maybe?" Mateo asks. "So hot today. It'd be faster with two."

"Sure," I tell him. "I'm just about finished here."

"Excellent. I'll help you pack up."

We slide the soil samples into a case, stash the tools in the back of the Jeep where it's parked at the edge of the persimmon plot, and drive toward the almond grove. The almonds are at the opposite end of the eighty acres, and I'm relieved for the light wind as we bounce across the uneven ground along the orchard's edge. The almond trees have had no water for months as we force them to weather the drought. When I stand among them, I can feel their bodies withering even as they stubbornly continue to produce flower and fruit among yellowing clusters of leaves.

When we arrive at the grove, I sit a moment longer while Mateo unloads the supplies. When he eyes me with concern, I smile, quickly lower myself from the Jeep into the dry grass. The temperature has climbed into the upper 90s, making this the perfect time of day to measure the water potential: when it is hottest and driest, creating the maximum stress for the plants. I steady myself, let a moment of vertigo pass as Mateo checks the equipment. Then, in tandem, Mateo and I test the water tension in the trees.

I start out ahead, select one leaf from each tree—shaded and low down, close in—and slide a little foil bag around it. To get an accurate stem water potential reading, each leaf is enclosed for ten minutes to allow it to equilibrate with the water-conducting system in the trunk. Mateo follows behind to take the readings, clipping the leaves and placing them into the pressure chamber.

The first time I learned to use the chamber, I struggled to work the pump, my arms so unmuscled and thin. The device was staked into the ground, and I grasped the waist-level handles, using all my strength to raise and lower the compression tube in an action similar to inflating a bike tire. I watched the bars on the gauge rise with each effort, about half a bar per pump. Ten bars, twelve, fifteen. Inside my bones, I could feel the trees around me pulling water from the soil, working to draw it up toward their yearning leaves. When I looked through the magnifying lens and finally saw the water bubbling out of the compressed petiole, I felt spent. As if the stress the trees were under was my own. My hands shook as I opened the chamber, released the leaf.

Now, I hold an almond leaf gently between my fingers, tuck it carefully into the little bag, and press the seal closed around the stem. I try to ignore the pinch in my throat, a growing tightness in my chest. I put my hand on the tree's trunk, its bark rough beneath my sweating skin. Sometimes it seems these roots could devour me whole, so desperate are they for anything to quench their thirst.

I think of Persephone, sent again and again beneath the earth. Whether deceived or chosen, Persephone's power over her own destiny was forever forfeit. She was told where to go, who to be with. How many days a year she could lay eyes on the sun. How many other days her body and her divinity were not her own, no matter how many lost souls called her their queen.

Six pomegranate seeds. Each red morsel rupturing between her teeth and tongue.

There were years when I, too, chained my body to the underworld's gates. Years with my hands on the teats of goats, a pail of warm milk at my feet, and tasting none of it. Years of my mother's fresh-baked bread, butter churned by my father's hands, and me barely nibbling at the crusts while my brothers smeared strawberry jam across their noisy mouths. One bite might doom me to nothingness, or one bite might be the thing to keep me aboveground.

I can hear Mateo gaining on me, the sound of the pump going up and down: the clank of the small metal piston, the compressor's hiss. I take my hand off the trunk, step back into the mid-day sun. There are ten more trees left in the row, ten more almonds suffering in the dust. The little foil bags in my hand reflect the light, throw it back skyward. Mateo looks up at me from the chamber's lens. Has he noticed how I have lost weight again? How I am faltering?

"All good over there, Sharon?"

My name lilting with an alveolar trill. Just the merest hint of a breeze.

I give Mateo a thumbs up, notice how my finger bones surface in my skin.

At the next tree, I let my body rest against the twisting trunk. I fold the selected leaf tenderly, like I'm swaddling it for an afternoon nap. Sometimes these days, when I'm standing in the orchard alone, I'm overwhelmed by the flesh of the stubborn fruits. Apricots firm as the knobs of my elbows, figs mimicking the modest slope of my breasts. The skin of my neck seems dusky as prunes, my cheeks round as nectarines. But the sensation is fleeting, and my cheeks sink back into my gums.

I can see it now, how my body is wasting, a familiar and somehow inevitable lessening. But when I was a teenager, I could not. I ate next to nothing, wished for more and more of myself to disappear. My sophomore year of high school, I collapsed in science class, test tubes clattering about me onto the floor. The hospital was horrible, all of it. So many machines. Nothing that resembled food. Worse when my parents were at my bedside, failing to hide their disapproval.

It was the trees that sustained me. The poplars and willows that formed the shelterbelt of our farm. Sitting beneath them, my blood felt rich, my limbs strong. As their branches filled with leaves that summer, I willed my body to take what was offered. I forced myself to eat a soft-boiled egg, take a bite of my father's homemade goat cheese spread across a wedge of dark bread. Savored those earthy flavors in my mouth, letting them keep me here, in the world of the living. My brothers sent to muck out the barn while my mother thrust a spoon into my emaciated hand.

"Hey, Sharon!"

Mateo's voice is urgent, higher pitched. I turn to see him just two trees down, bent over and staring hard at the bar gauge, hands tight around the handles of the pressure chamber.

"What is it? Is something wrong?"

I know there is. I can feel it as a brittleness in my bones, a tension in the muscles of my chest.

"Look at this. Have you ever seen the bars this high?"

With the conditions we subject these trees to, we sometimes see the gauge rise to 50, 60 bars. But this reading is rising toward 200, threatening to fall off the gauge completely. Trees this stressed shouldn't even be alive, much less producing almonds too numerous for us to count.

"It must be a mistake," I say, reaching to pluck the bagged leaf off the next tree down. "Let's try another one." Usually, the leaves snap off easily, the stem bending back at the nap. But I can feel the tree refusing, trying to hang on to what belongs to it.

Drought-resistant trees, like the original pistachios, produce tiny fruit. But some of the trees we're breeding in the orchard are Frankensteins. They have rootstocks engineered to withstand drought, or tolerate salt. Then on top, we graft a species that will yield large, delicious fruits. This is what the commercial farmers want. This is what will feed the warming world. But these two-souled trees, divided like Persephone, can they recognize themselves any longer?

Often during the long days in grad school, lost in stacks of books or holed up in the lab, I would forget to eat. Mateo would draw me out, lead me to the trees. He and I would walk through the orchard together at dusk, the sun reddening in its descent, casting ochre light through rows. In early autumn, the evening air took on a chill, and the stone fruits of the hardiest specimens hung ripe among the leaves. Together, we would pull down the globes of fruit and pile them against our chests. The trees were always generous. We'd sit against the trunks and bite into peaches, kiwifruit, and plums. In the dwindling light, we'd lick the juice off our sticky fingers, suck every morsel from the pits. Wresting the stubborn leaf from the branch now, I stare at my thin hands and wonder how they can possibly be my own.

We drop the new leaf into the chamber, secure the pins. As Mateo begins to pump, I can feel the breath leaving my lungs. My mouth goes dry. Up and down, up and down, Mateo works the pump, waiting for the petiole to give up its water. The rows of almonds blur. The sun is at its highest, relentless. The world is spinning. I stumble backwards, lean my body against the nearest trunk.

"Sharon?"

As if from a great distance, Mateo's voice filters through the sun-scorched leaves. He lets go of the pressure chamber, moves towards me.

I slide suddenly down against the base of the tree, smack my head on its buttresses. There is a deep rumble beneath the orchard, and I can feel the angry roots of the trees stirring. A tremor, and then the ground opens up between Mateo and me. A crack in the dry earth that splits the aisle of almond trees in two.

My face in the dirt. The nickering of horses.

My parents' faces hover over me, then are trampled in a slurry of pigs and goats. Somewhere, the voices of my brothers throw my name into the hot wind.

Mateo calls out to me across the growing divide. "Sharon!"

Beneath the earth, an underworld of skeletal root systems. A rising of the dead. Someone is coming toward me through the haze of dust.

"Sharon!"

Pressure builds inside my head. A terrible thirst puckers my skin. My arms: a spindle of branching. All around me, the bodies of trees, their beautiful fruits. And there is Persephone, tender and fierce as a new bud in spring. A pomegranate seed balanced between her finger and thumb.

Animal Rain

They knew their relationship was finally over the day frogs fell out of the sky. As they sat together in the breakfast nook on a summer Saturday, she was spreading marmalade on her toast—too much, he thought, considering the little jar was nearly empty—and he looked down at his own naked toast and hated her for the third time since they'd woken up. She smeared the marmalade with her knife so it mixed with the butter in a complex marbling that was a cheery counterpoint to the lack of sun outside. Gray clouds gathered across the horizon, and she was thinking about how she loved Iowa's thunderstorms more than she loved him.

She could feel his eyes on her as she slathered her toast, but she couldn't bring herself to care about how much was left. She set the marmalade jar down but did not pass it to him.

"Do you think there will be hail?" she asked. She loved hail, despite the fact that during the last big storm it had pelted her hatchback and left a dot-to-dot of little dents across the roof. She thought of it as a sort of reverse braille, a message to run her fingers across each time she stood next to her car waiting for him, trying to decide if it was telling her to stay or go. He was always late coming out of his office, but she continued to pick him up because it was on her way home from the library where she worked, and he didn't have a car. They had moved here, away from her beloved ocean, for him to pursue a tenure track position at the university. It didn't work out, but here they still were, landlocked and buried under his student loans.

He reached for the marmalade jar, which was unpleasantly sticky on the sides. He no longer found her haphazardness charming. Or her fondness for unpleasant weather. "Maybe," he said, keeping the annoyance out of his voice. Instead, he made a lot of noise with his knife as he tried to extract enough marmalade to cover his cooling toast. The sky darkened alongside his mood.

"I hope so," she said. "You know how much I like dramatic weather on days I don't have to leave the house."

The weather was always more dramatic than they were. They didn't fight, at least not out loud. She had long, involved arguments with him inside her head. A thousand illuminating and important things that she would never say to him. He concentrated on any manner of distractions: video games, his phone, the TV. He pretended he didn't hear her, even when she wasn't talking to him.

They had been married nine years. Long enough that it was hard to let go. Long enough that neither of them wanted to admit failure, or think about the daunting prospect of finding someone else, or being alone. They couldn't remember which books were whose. Did the vinyl collection belong to both of them equally? They didn't have kids, which was something. But who would get the cat?

She looked out the window, the sky a roil of graphite and midnight blue. "You're not going anywhere today, are you? Looks like tornado weather." It wasn't that she didn't care about him. That was what made it so hard to think about leaving. She didn't want to be with him, but she also couldn't bear to imagine him with anyone else. Either way, she didn't want him to be caught in the middle of a storm.

"No," he said, unable to think of any place he had an excuse to go. It was so dark outside it didn't look like morning anymore. He thought of how weekends had been with her, in the beginning. They used to spend whole days in bed, not knowing or caring what time it might be. The weather outside didn't matter. Everything he needed to know about heat and sweat, deluge and shiver, was contained in the rise of her hips, the lightning-spark of her fingers. Her thick hair flooding across his bare chest. His head resting on her slick collarbone as he listened to the soft thrum of her heart.

"Look!" Her mouth full of toast, it came out garbled. She stood up from the table and pointed out the window. "What is *that*?"

He looked at her hand, the slightness and stickiness of it. The bands that nested on her ring finger, simple and diamondless, graced instead by a small sapphire that mirrored the complicated blue of her eyes. He followed the line of her finger past the window and down the empty block. An angry churn of clouds was dropping some sort of muddied hail onto the careful lawns, the smooth suburban street.

"I have no idea," he said, squinting out at the cloud-shadowed street.

That's not normal rain, she thought. And it's not hail, either.

She pressed her hand against the windowpane, leaned her face close to the glass. Sometimes a storm meant danger, and she knew to stay away from windows, head for the basement, hunker down. But there were no tornado sirens. No winds thrashing the sides of the house. Just a muffled *thwack thwack thwack* of weighty precipitation hitting the ground.

They were silent together, which wasn't unusual. He watched as she left marmalade prints on the glass. For a moment, he wanted to lift her hand to his lips, lick her fingers clean. When was the last time he had tasted her skin?

"I'm going out there," she said.

"Wait," he said. "I'll go with you."

She turned to him, saw the brief flicker of longing in his face. When they first moved to Iowa, they would walk along the Mississippi, watch the riverboats with their brightly lit paddlewheels in the dusk. She remembered her fingers laced through his, the electric brush of his shoulder against hers. How she never grew cold. Now, they barely touched. Slept turned away from each other. Rarely looked into one another's eyes.

"OK," she said.

She opened the door, and they walked barefoot onto the porch.

The sound was a sickening *splat splat* on the asphalt, louder now that they were outside. The humid air slunk up their arms, beaded on the backs of their necks. As they crossed the lawn and stepped into the street, dozens of small, green bodies exploded on the pavement around their bare toes. The frogs that survived the impact kicked their outspread legs, as if struggling to swim. Horrified, he covered his head with his arms. She regarded him with disappointment, then stared sadly at the frog-laden cloud.

"We should go back inside," he said, as a slippery, doomed body ricocheted off his elbow. But she didn't move. The street was a bright palette of amphibious remains.

Is this what we have come to? he thought, wincing as another frog shattered at his feet. He wished he could pull her to him, fix whatever had gone wrong between them. In the early years of their marriage, he had always been able to soften her with a joke, or a touch: twin tethers that coaxed her into his arms. Now his head was crowded with all the wrong words, his hands empty.

He remembered how, on their last night before coming to Iowa, they had gone down to the ocean as the tide was receding. The beach was littered with stranded sand dollars, the fuzzy discs of their shells half-burrowed into the wet shore. She had stopped to pick one up, placed it in his hand so he could feel how it was still alive. Its tiny spines moved against his skin. Then she took it back gently and returned it to the water, the waves drawing it out to sea.

Neighbors were stationed at windows, watching from dry, unmarred rooms. One teenager switchbacked down the block with a lacrosse net, shouting for help as he tried to intercept frogs before they hit the ground. She seemed rooted in place. Some days, she hardly resembled the person he married. How could she be so calm in the midst of such messy dying?

"Should we do something?" he asked.

She felt a small pull toward him, the overlapping kindness and helplessness in his voice. But she knew there was no point in trying to save anything.

"It's not that uncommon," she said.

He watched her from beneath the umbrella of his arms, the rain of frogs beginning to slow. He was never surprised when she knew something strange. He had come to appreciate her librarian brain, full of eclectic facts. "Oh?" he said.

"Animal rain." She didn't look at him, her eyes still skyward. "Small animals can get swept up in waterspouts when a storm passes over a body of water. It pulls them into the funnel cloud. Can carry them for miles." Her heart felt heavy in her chest, nebulous.

"I think we should go inside," he said again. "If there's nothing to be done."

Yes, she thought, it's too late. But she didn't say it.

Neighbors were venturing outside, inspecting their yards and sidewalks, crumpling up their noses and mouths. The two of them stood there as fewer and fewer frogs dropped back to the earth. And then she held out her hands in front of her, cupped together, palms up.

As he watched, one of the last falling bodies landed in her waiting hands. She lowered her head to look at it. He took a step closer, careful to avoid the unfortunate frogs at his feet, and let his arms rest at his sides.

A stunned leopard frog sat unmoving in the bowl of her palms. It was varying shades of mossy green, covered with a random array of round, black spots. Two light-colored ridges extended from its startled eyes down its vapor-wet back. It held perfectly still, unblinking, the white pouch of its chin pulsating with rapid breaths.

"I think it's over," he said, the black clouds thinning to deep gray.

"Yes," she said, out loud. "I think it is."

Their eyes found each other above the body of the little frog as it began to shift and turn circles in her hands.

"What should we do?" He felt a tightening in his throat, a painful relief in his chest.

She smiled at him, didn't hold back her tears. The weight of the frog was almost nothing. "You can have the cat," she said.

The frog gave a guttural, rattling croak, the sides of its throat expanding. He looked away from her beautiful, weeping face, down at the creature's restless eyes.

She turned from him, folded the frog between her hands, and carried it away from the splattered street. The grass of their neatly-trimmed lawn was sharp on the soles of her feet. Small pocks of mud glistened where he had pulled up all the dandelions. As the rain started up, the little frog squirmed in the dark pocket of her palms. A low roll of thunder sounded in the distance as she crouched down in the grass and let it go.

The Care Home

"She's keeping everyone awake, Dana." It's six o'clock on an already warm summer morning, and our newest resident's chart is spread out before us on the desk. We've never taken in a banshee before, and we're searching for clues as to what might calm her. Orlagh's wails pulse at an otherworldly volume through the farmhouse, surging down the hallway to where Dana and I sit in the tiny office. Our degrees and certificates rattle on the walls in their wooden frames. "I don't know what we were thinking."

"We'll figure it out, Tenley. We always do." Dana seems unphased by the deafening screeches as she sits across from me and shuffles through piles of cryptic notes. "Remember when we took in the Gorgon?"

I do. Avoiding the Gorgon's head of serpents was one thing. But we had to earn her trust without looking at her, or risk being turned to stone.

Dana raises her voice so I can hear her better over the wails, even though we are only a couple of feet apart. "I mean, that wasn't easy, but we managed. Eventually."

Dana is the optimist, the problem solver. This home was her idea. I had just inherited the farmhouse and its thousand-acre plot of land from my grandparents, and Dana's vision was the perfect project to pull me out of my grief. Together we created a place for the most dreadful of women to live out their lives, away from the cruelties of the larger world. Except we don't think they're dreadful. They're trapped in the stories that have been told about them, passed down from nightmare to nightmare, generation to generation. Until we came along ten years ago and started bringing them here.

Dana and I met in med school. We were drawn to each other by our mutual passion for Mythic rights. Why beings like our residents continue to be referred to as Mythics even after their discovery by ordinary humans is a point of contention, as it's obvious they actually exist. And could crush us with godlike ease if they chose. But there are so few of them left, and they usually prefer to go unnoticed. The ones who come to live with us are either nearing the end of their lives or are deemed too dangerous (or inconvenient) for the human-dominated world.

And while Orlagh's howls are unnerving, Agnes—the Gorgon—was even more challenging to care for. It was so easy for her to do away with someone, whether on purpose or by accident. Agnes was one of our earliest residents, coming to us just a few months after we finished the renovations to the farmhouse. Dana and I had recently completed our residencies, young doctors brimming with ideas for changing the world. But we were struggling through a steep learning curve, figuring out how to run this kind of home. I don't know of a single med school that includes a class in the care of (so-called) "mythological beasts".

We don't use that word around here, beasts. These are women, even if they don't look or act the way most folks think they should.

Agnes had been holed up in a cave when the Gatherers found her, so old her limbs were as twisted as the venomous creatures on her head. She was traumatized by decades of isolation, and we questioned whether she could make the transition to group living. Even at her advanced age, she was dangerous, unpredictable. The Gatherers had bound her for travel, covered her eyes with a thick cloth after several well-meaning others hardened during her capture, their earthen bodies frozen mid-struggle.

But Agnes's blindfold came loose upon her arrival, and she immediately turned one of our orderlies to stone. Dana and I felt his solidification as our failure, sent all the other employees away while we dealt with her ourselves. With our eyes shut tight, we kept Agnes restrained while we convinced her to let us close enough to examine her body, catalog her myriad scars. I still feel badly about doing this. We try not to force any of the women who come here to do anything, to have anything done to them. It's better if they give over their wounds themselves.

Once Agnes understood we wanted to help her, she settled down. The snakes stopped hissing, coiled up in quiet rings against her scalp. She requested sunglasses, eventually asked to be at the breakfast table with the others. She was graceful, witty, well-read. All she wanted was to eat her French toast without some hotheaded lug of a hero barging through her door with a sword.

Agnes grew accustomed to her new living situation, was fond of her fellow residents. But with her age came moments of confusion. After she mistakenly turned one of our nurses to stone in a temporary state of disorientation in the middle of the night, Agnes withdrew, refused to leave her room. I think she knew it was only a matter of time before she accidentally petrified everyone in the home. In the end—despite our near-constant attentiveness—she blinded herself with a butter knife. After that, she spent the rest of her days lounging in the common room swapping war stories with the other women, her snakes growing long and docile, resting their ruby-eyed heads on her strong, scarred shoulders.

I pull an x-ray out of a manila folder, hold it up to the window so the dawn light silhouettes an amorphous form. "I'm sure you're right, Dana. We'll be able to help Orlagh. It's just hard to think with all the screaming." Even after a decade of experience, we never feel completely equipped to take in an unfamiliar resident, but the Gatherers insisted there was nowhere else for Orlagh to go.

Living with us now are Ardith (succubus), Thea (harpy), and Molpe (siren). Orlagh arrived just after dinner last night, and everyone tried to make her feel welcome. Thea and Molpe made cookies. Ardith hung garlands of wildflowers around the common room. Dana and I prepared Orlagh's bedroom with soft linens, new cotton pillows. Laid out a comb with a carved bone handle for her hair. But we were utterly unprepared for the magnitude of grief that walked through our door.

The ear-piercing howls are beyond what I could have imagined. Orlagh's voice is like a being unto itself, barreling through the thin walls of the house, crashing into everything. Though she doesn't appear to be in physical pain, she won't talk to us, won't speak about whatever's happening. She just cries and cries, inconsolable. Nobody has gotten any sleep. This morning, everyone seems as perplexed as Dana and I are about what to do for Orlagh. The cook and day nurses have not yet arrived, and while we pore over the files, the other women have retreated to a far corner of the garden, the rising sun glinting off the feathers of three very different sets of wings.

All manner of women have lived with us over the years. There was Cora, a selkie who came to us after being rescued from a circus. She split her time between the house and an inflatable pool in the backyard, depending on which skin she was in. But her longing for the sea was too strong, and we eventually asked the Gatherers to arrange for her safe passage from our farm to the waters around Nova Scotia.

Then there was the vampire. With Ecaterina, it was all about helping her learn to control her cravings and develop a healthy relationship with food. I had an arrangement with a local slaughterhouse, and we were able to wean her off human blood and onto that of pigs and cows. I used to show up at the bleeding zone once a week with an armful of empty milk jugs.

People around here have known me since I was a child. I visited my grandparents often, and they'd take me on their rounds as they stopped in on neighbors or went into town for supplies. When my grandparents died, the locals stepped up to make sure I had what I needed. They helped me fix up the farmhouse, brought tools and paint and lumber, the gift of their time and expertise. I've learned they'll do anything for me. And they've come to appreciate the services we provide at the home. How we keep the peace.

As to our current residents, Thea and Molpe were nearly inseparable from the start, what with both of them being half-bird. They came to us at the same time, on the run from the local sheriff. Thea was caught stealing fresh salmon from a farmer's market, and Molpe had racked up multiple charges of assault against a host of men, but every instance sounded more like self-defense.

Though we almost never get visitors out here, on the rare occasion nosy detectives or anti-Mythics do show up, Thea conjures winds that put tornados and hurricanes to shame. She whips up a storm to carry intruders away, past the miles of wheat fields and pockets of forest, above herds of grazing cows she leaves unscathed. Once the unwelcome folks have been deposited elsewhere, Thea summons the winds back to her and swallows their raging breath, sucks them down into the feathered plexus of her chest.

Until she met Thea, Molpe preferred that trespassers not be spared, even if she had lured them herself. She loves to serenade us with tales of shipwrecks, men whose advances she could not abide. Landlocked as Molpe is now, and free to practice her art without an unwanted audience, she spends afternoons in the garden composing melodies with Thea, attracting only songbirds. Finches, sparrows, and thrushes gather above them in the trees. Wrens and starlings perch on the fence posts and join in. Harpy and siren roost together, humming softly as they preen each other's feathers.

Thea and Molpe took Ardith under their wings as soon as they heard her story: how the man she had been living with raged at her until she did whatever he asked, beat her if she tried to refuse. Then he locked her up in a cabin, deep in the forest. The night she tricked him into removing the chains from her wrists and ankles, she flew straight up through the roof, splintering the cedar shingles as she went. He tried to shoot her down with a rifle, but she had already ascended beyond his reach. She flew until she found our farm, drawn by Thea and Molpe's singing.

The women here look out for one another. I'm sure they want to comfort Orlagh, but no one seems to know how. I feel the vibration of her shrieks in every part of my body, like her sorrow might shatter us if we can't ease her anguish.

I pass the x-ray over to Dana. "Look there." I point at the middle of the scan, below what I think are ribs, at something that doesn't appear to be a normal organ. The image is so blurry it's not of much use, but I can hardly blame the technicians. Women like Orlagh are often hard to photograph, even in the best of circumstances. "What do you think that is?"

Dana holds the x-ray up to the window again, squinting through her glasses and leaning closer. "Huh. I don't know. Could be a tumor. It would be just like the Gatherers not to give us the full story."

The Gatherers are the source of many of our residents. They're part mythologist, part tracker, part social worker. An unusual skill set, to be sure. They're also notoriously cagey. But we're grateful for their work, and for their partnership with our facility. Until we opened the home, women like Orlagh would end up institutionalized, or worse, depending on the area where they were discovered. That practice didn't sit right with Dana or me. I only wish we could take in more than four at a time. Maybe someday. Right now, I'm beginning to doubt our abilities as Orlagh's wails reverberate around the office walls. Luckily the closest neighbor is two miles away.

Orlagh had been living largely unnoticed in a small, rural town. She had kept to herself, worked her garden, tended to an ever-growing pack of stray dogs. No one knew she was a banshee until the night her keening began. The dogs had joined in, howling through the night, standing guard at her door. The Gatherers had to be careful when they came to collect her, as the dogs clearly didn't want to let her go. They brought Orlagh to the local hospital first, but the staff refused to keep her there past her initial exam. A space in the home had just opened up as Ceridwyn, our resident wraith, had an epiphany and decided to cross over. So Orlagh came to us.

"A tumor is possible." I move around the desk to look at the x-ray over Dana's shoulder. "It's hard to tell what's going on from this worthless scan. I don't know. Maybe this is just normal banshee behavior?"

Usually, a banshee's keening would herald the death of a family member. We have no idea if Orlagh has any relations. The Gatherers only brought the words of a few neighbors and this small stack of medical charts. And we have no prior experience with banshees. What their x-rays should look like, how long their crying lasts, or how to make it stop.

"We need to try to talk to her again." Dana stands up and gives my arm a tug. "Come on."

When we step out of the office, Ardith is waiting in the hallway. Her hands are cupped over her ears, elbows pointed down to avoid her heavy spiral horns. Ardith's wings are folded neatly against her back, their leathery tips hooding her shoulders. Her hooves peek out from under her long floral sundress, and her pointed tail rests on the floor. She did away with her more provocative succubus attire long ago, after what happened.

When Ardith first came to us, she could barely speak. She lay curled on her bed, her arms wrapped around her chest, hiding beneath the cocoon of her wings. When she finally allowed us near, we could see she was covered in bruises. Fresh cuts. Old scars. She was lucky to have escaped. Brave to leave him. It took her a long time to realize he would never find her here, that she was safe with us. Thea and Molpe spent many hours at Ardith's bedside, singing to her. Their songs both held her pain, and banished it. Ardith came back to herself, found her voice again through theirs.

"Ardith." I touch her shoulder. "I'm sorry about the noise. I know it's upsetting."

Ardith shakes her head and takes her hands off her ears, her green, glowing eyes full of kindness. "Can I go with you to see Orlagh?" she asks. "Please?"

Dana doesn't hesitate. "Of course." We know from experience that these women are often each other's best medicine.

Orlagh's room is at the other end of the farmhouse, in a hallway off the kitchen. Her shrieks are growing louder and more intense. As we approach, Ardith steps ahead of us and lays her hand on the knob. She takes a deep breath. We all do. And then she opens the door.

Orlagh is sitting in her bed, leaning against the headboard. Her body is electric with sound, eyes bloodshot and terrified, long, dark hair levitating away from her skin. Her hands sprawl over her belly, her fingers interlaced in knots.

Ardith hurries to her, Dana and I close behind. Something is clearly wrong. More wrong than before. Orlagh is straining now, her whole body tense. I reach out my hand toward her, then hesitate, wanting her to consent to my touch. Her eyes are red from weeping, wide with sorrow, but they find mine, and she doesn't resist. I brush aside her wild hair, lay my hand on her forehead. She's sweating, but not with fever. Dana lifts Orlagh's wrist to take her pulse, but her hand immediately springs back to her belly. The room crackles with screaming.

Ardith places her hands on Orlagh's abdomen as it tightens and relaxes, and then she looks up at us. "I think she's in labor."

"Labor?" I stare at Dana, who looks as confused as I am. If Orlagh is pregnant, she's not far along enough to show. How could the hospital have missed such a thing? How could we?

I remember the x-ray, the unusual shape beneath Orlagh's ribs.

Level-headed as always, Dana shouts over the cacophonous drone. "Tenley, I'm going to get some supplies."

Ardith has pried one of Orlagh's hands from her contracting belly and holds it within her own. It's hot in the room, so Ardith spreads her wings, enormous and gentle, and fans Orlagh to keep her cool.

I open the window and find Thea and Molpe standing outside, leaning their heads together, looking in. They appear to me as a two-headed woman, bare breasted and open hearted, light curls interwoven with dark, all their varied feathers shimmering in the sun. They are ancient, and I imagine they have seen everything. But perhaps not this: a laboring banshee attended by a succubus and two humans who are used to ushering lives out of the world, not into it.

"Orlagh," I say, as I crouch down next to her beautiful, contorted face. "I'm going to have a look between your legs."

She nods the slightest of discernable nods and bends her legs up to her chest as I kneel at the end of the bed. Dana is back, at my side with water and towels, and the two of us lift the mossy green fabric of Orlagh's dress. The sheets underneath are stained with blood.

Out here in the middle of nowhere, we are all these women have. All Orlagh has on this summer morning as her insides try to turn themselves out. Two doctors and three winged women watching over her, none of us angels. And none of us knows what comes next.

We don't have to wait long. Orlagh draws in a huge, gasping breath, and on her moan of an exhale, a small being slips out of her into my waiting hands.

The wailing stops, and the room feels much too quiet. A staccato triple chirp of a magpie sounds in the distance. Dana draws a wet cloth across the infant's face to clear the blood, but already I know what Orlagh has known all along. The baby—so, so little, several months premature—is cold and still in my palms.

Orlagh's breathing is heavy and uneven. Ardith shifts her wings upward, out of the way, and climbs into the bed next to Orlagh, who slumps against her. Ardith strokes Orlagh's long, tangled hair, lays her cheek on top of the banshee's head. My ears are ringing as Dana takes the dead child from my hands.

As all the women watch, Dana slowly immerses the baby in the bowl of water, carefully cleans its blue-gray skin. Its lips are dark red, almost black. Its fingers and toes are the size of beans. Dana pats the small body dry, wraps it in a clean towel.

As Dana hands the baby to Orlagh, she begins to keen again. But deep and low this time, a sound I can feel right in the center of my chest. When one of our residents dies, we have a ritual. We gather at night to bless the transformed woman, honor her body—however harmed or misunderstood—with our touch. We build a pyre, give her over to the darkness and the stars. No one asks the details of what we do out here, of how residents come and go. They are only glad not to have to live among these women.

But today's death is different. This little one never had a chance to take on the evils of the world, to soften or transform them. Ardith enfolds Orlagh within her wings, rocking her and the tiny stillborn child. Dana grabs hold of my hand, and the two of us stand there at the end of the bed, witness to all we cannot mend. Above Orlagh's keening, another sound strengthens, haunting and ethereal. The melody rises into the summer's insect noise and trilling birds as the harpy and the siren offer up their song.

The Ghost Town Collectives

A fright. That's what you're supposed to call a group of ghosts. Not a herd. Not a flock. Not some sort of harmless congregation of beings. A fright of ghosts. As if fear is the only option. That there would be no room in your heart, in your body, for anything else, were you to come upon them. Were they to come upon you. But there are other possibilities. Like the year Liam McDaniel turned 51 and found his way to an abandoned mountain town in Colorado, the aspen trees just beginning to clatter into a warm and golden autumn. You know what year it was. The year everyone he loved most died.

Liam's circumstances were unusual for their raw improbability. Perhaps you understand this from within circumstances of your own. You know Liam, sympathize with his loss. Perhaps you lost someone, too. Maybe your wife died. Your husband, your partner. The person whose hand you held within yours for years, or whose hand you had only just begun to hold, already feeling how it could last. Maybe your parents died, either at the end of long lives or not so long. Maybe you lost a child. A grown child, or a baby, or one who was at that in between age: not too young to take notice but not old enough to understand. Or maybe you were already alone, but before you didn't mind so much, and now you do. Or maybe you always minded. You always had that ache in your chest. Whatever your circumstance, you know what it's like to keep company with absence in an empty room.

A group of patients is called a virtue. A group of doctors is called a doctrine. There is no definitive collective noun for corpses. There are many names for a group of trees. A clump, a forest, a coupe. A grove. A thicket. A stillness. A stand.

After everyone he loved most had died, after he couldn't touch them while they were dying, and after he also couldn't touch anyone else he knew—those who might have loved him or he might have come to love—Liam McDaniel left everything to be among the trees. A stillness of trees. A place where being alone was a choice, not something that happened to you while you tried to push it away. After everyone he loved most had died, Liam read an article about a man who bought a ghost town. It was a hopeful story. The man bought the ghost town before the virus crossed the ocean, crossed every state line. While the man was visiting his ghost town, the order came to shelter in place. So the man hunkered down, discovered treasures in all of the ghost town's walls. It was a hopeful story. The man was having the time of his life.

A group of bats is called a colony. There is no designation for a group of viruses. Perhaps because it only takes one. One virus that jumps from its usual host. An infection. An outbreak. An epidemic. A pandemic.

Liam had held his wife's hands in his hands, and then he hadn't. His wife's hands had been strong, her nails trimmed short. She made things with paint and she made things with rope and wool and she made things with clay and she made things with metal and stone. Once she made the shell of a person that you could step inside of. Like a papier-mâché mask, but life-size, cast from head to toe. You were the skeleton. You were the organs—the lungs and heart. Your breath was warm coming through the nostrils of the face. You could hear, and you could see through the holes of its eyes, but you were fixed in place and couldn't move. When it was exhibited, people in galleries revolved around the shell to see who might be standing inside. To take their turns being inside. Everyone was allowed to touch.

A group of houses is called a huddle. There is no word for a group of ghost towns, but they are littered throughout the Colorado mountains. Liam found a listing for one that was headed to auction— just a single cabin still standing, the remains of a saloon, the small dark opening of a mine against the rocky earth—disintegrating in an alpine meadow. Sitting in the empty kitchen of his house, one among the huddle of little brick houses whose windows reflected Denver's late summer sun, Liam placed his empty hands palms up on the table's dark wood. He stared at his left hand and imagined it pooling with blood, imagined the deep line of a wound across his wrist. Liam had no parents left to miss him. No wife who would find him. No children he could harm with his leaving. A group of children is called an ingratitude. But there are other possibilities.

Liam stared at his right hand, and no matter how hard he tried, he couldn't see it as completely empty. Light spilled through the kitchen windows, filled the cup of his palm. If he turned his palm over, the light was stubborn, flickered on the back of his hand. Reached all the way up to his elbow, hot and bright. It was not a ghost. But Liam didn't know that then. He hadn't yet seen the real thing. The light was not the ghost of his wife or the ghosts of his children. It was just an abundance of sunlight with exceptional timing. Liam chose his right hand and used it to call up the real estate agent and place his bid.

*****

A group of carpenters is called a panel. A group of architects is called a rendering. A group of sculptors is a mold. Liam's wife had built spectacular things out of ordinary things, pieces of things, while Liam's hands drafted plans, then carried them out with nails and screws and joists and planks and beams. Liam's hands had been over every inch of their brick bungalow, working its pieces until the house was distinctively theirs. He had mended pipes and shored up sinking porch columns and restored the built-in cabinetry with sandpaper and stain and sweat. He had painted bedrooms. Painted nurseries. Painted the kitchen with its riot of light. And within the house's walls, Liam's hands had been over every inch of his wife. Had tended his children when they were newborns hollering at the middle-of-night moon.

Though you might have thought otherwise, Liam wasn't afraid of ghosts or the prospect of living in a ghost town. As he prepared to leave the bungalow, he moved room to room, accounting for the accumulation of things by trying to see with his wife's eyes. Noting how each item might have a use. How it might become something new. But then he packed up most of the contents of the house to put in storage while he was away. He set aside very few things to bring with him. The wooden box his daughter had made last year in high school wood shop, because that was how he knew she had inherited his hands. The ceramic serving bowl his son had recently made in pottery class, because that was how he knew those hands were gifts from his wife. The shell of a person his wife had made and exhibited many times, but never sold. The rest of what he took from the house fit easily into the back of his pickup truck. There were no ghosts, so the ghosts took up no space at all.

Liam drove away from the little brick house, away from the huddle of brick houses, through the crisscross of city streets and out of the city altogether. A group of maps is called a latitude. A group of mountains is called a range. Liam followed the maps into the mountains, drove until the highways turned to roads and the roads turned to dirt and tailings and dead-ended in the meadow of his ghost town, ringed with aspen trees glittering in the mid-September sun. When Liam stepped out of his truck, the alpine air raised up goosebumps on his skin, and then the sun smoothed them down again. The aspen trees shivered their cymbals of leaves all around him. Liam sank to his knees in the scrub-brown grass, wrapped his arms about himself, and began to cry. There is no agreed upon name for a collective of tears.

*****

One thing you should know about ghosts is that they rarely waste time. Another is that they are rarely direct. Anything caught between worlds exists with both urgency and uncertainty. Liam could feel the expectant energy in the air, nudging him to get settled before dark. So he rose from his knees and walked across the meadow toward the cabin. Dozens of grasshoppers zig-zagged through the last of the summer's fading wildflowers, bumping into his legs and springing away. The first living creatures to touch him in months. He stumbled a little, startled by the proximity of their bodies, but then leaned into them, trying to catch them between his hands. A group of grasshoppers is called a cloud. A cloud of grasshoppers, moving across the brilliant blue sky, out of Liam's reach.

Standing in front of the little cabin, Liam with his architect's mind marveled at its longevity. It was constructed of carefully saddle-notched, hand-sawed logs, its windows uncannily intact. Liam tested the door, reinforced with tin to deter rodents, and found that it still hinged open and closed, that it could be secured by a wooden peg fitted in a hasp. The shallow pitch of the roof, crafted from a sturdy ridge log and purlins and wedged with collar ties beneath the eaves, explained the years the cabin had survived beneath heavy snow. Liam ran his carpenter's hands along the unpeeled logs. A masterful example of vernacular architecture, wrought with hand tools from materials nearby. Liam wished he could have met the builder of this cabin, could have sat with him and watched summer thunderstorms roll in over the peaks as they drank strong coffee and wiped the dirt from their palms.

Liam's son had died first. Just a couple of weeks after turning thirteen. You remember how it was. At first we thought children were invincible, that the virus would inhabit them quietly and then go on its way. We took steps to protect the children, anyway. But a few days into the stay-at-home order, the first week that schools were closed, Liam's son developed a fever. After that, it was quick, like a boulder in a landslide, picking up speed as it tumbles through the scree. There is no standard collective noun for a group of rocks. Until they are stones, monuments set in place. A cairn of stones. A henge. Until they are gravestones, and then we don't know what to call them again. A cemetery is not a collection but a place, containing so much more than markers with names and dates. We might agree to call them by our own appellation: a grief of gravestones. A sorrow. But perhaps if we name death too precisely, we hold it too close.

Per hospital rules, children were not made to suffer alone as adults were, but only one parent was allowed to be at their son's bedside at a time. So Liam and his wife took shifts. When his wife called in the middle of the night as their son's body was failing, Liam could hear, through her sobs, the chaos of machines in the background. Long, high-pitched tones and alarms threaded themselves through her choked breaths, her urgent weeping. Liam hadn't been sleeping when she called. He had been standing in the dark kitchen, running his hand along the wooden doorframe. Wood that he had once restored to its original, flawless grain. He was trying to find comfort in that which had been tattered and then repaired. Liam was not there when his son died. It happened while he was racing through the quiet city toward the hospital, streetlights blurring into pinwheels through his watery eyes.

Liam stepped inside the little cabin. As his eyes adjusted to the interior dim, a table with two wooden chairs and a ladder to a sleeping loft came into focus. A cast iron wood stove hunkered in the corner of the single room. Something had chewed at the table legs—marmots, he suspected—and every surface was overspread with dirt and the scattered evidence of mice. The cabin's front window looked out over the meadow, across to the only other building left in Liam's ghost town—the remains of a saloon tilting into the afternoon light. But the saloon could wait. Liam unloaded his few belongings—the twin mattress that had been his daughter's, kitchen essentials, books, tools. One bundle of bedding. One large suitcase of clothes. Several bins of non-perishable food. The wooden box, the ceramic bowl, the human shell. One sturdy broom. Three small cremation boxes, each with a set of initials marked in Liam's scrupulous hand.

Liam swept away the dirt and droppings from the room and loft and secured the cabin door with the hasp. He hauled the mattress up the well-made ladder and fell into the heaviest sleep he'd had since everyone he loved most had died. Inside, a mischief of mice darted wall to wall in confusion. Outside, the aspen trees were alive in the wind. Perhaps all the creatures that roam about at night woke up. A mask of raccoons. A wiliness of coyotes. A crackle of crickets. A prickle of porcupines. A parliament of owls. Perhaps they moved in and out of the ghost town all night, around and around Liam's cabin, in and out of the bed of Liam's truck. Perhaps they were simply being exactly their animal selves, hunting and hiding in the darkness, smelling the new smell of Liam but leaving him be. But there are other possibilities.

*****

Liam was shaken out of sleep that first night by a sound like thunder. If not for the odor—a smell like a rodeo corral—he would have assumed a storm was preparing to heave the sky open, drench the meadow in late-summer rain. But the smell was overwhelming, dragged him fully out of sleep. The cabin was cold—he had been too exhausted to investigate the workability of the stove—and he wrapped himself in his blanket as he sat up. The walls and table were vibrating, the chairs making tiny jumps on the tremoring floor. Liam grabbed a camping lantern from his bedside, made his way down the ladder on careful bare feet.

Looking out the window, he saw them. Massive animals running together through the moon-bright meadow, their hooves rumbling over the open ground. Bison. A herd of bison plunging their earth-dark bodies through the grass, pressing the humps of their backs together as they ran, their horns shimmering in the lunar light. What was a herd of bison doing, traveling in the middle of the night? Liam bundled the blanket more tightly around him, slipped the peg from the hasp. As the door swung open, the sound and smell intensified, and Liam had to steady himself against the frame. These bison were enormous. Much larger than the ones he'd seen at the zoo. As he watched, the bison circled the meadow, drawing within a few yards of the cabin's door. And then, as Liam stepped back, the bison began to vanish, extinguished like streetlamps until a single bull stood at the far side of the meadow, its silhouette moonshadowed against the sagging wall of the saloon. The bull regarded Liam, lowered its gigantic head to snuff the ground, and then disappeared in a collapsing burst of light.

Liam blinked, then stared into the empty meadow. The air thickened with cricket noise and the rustling of aspen leaves. Was he dreaming? Had he finally succumbed to the fever, too, with its wild hallucinations? He set down the lantern, dropped the blanket behind him on the cabin floor, and stepped out barefoot into the meadow's grass. No hoofprints anywhere. The soil was utterly undisturbed. When everyone he loved most had died, no one could come to comfort Liam. No one could hold him in their arms. Friends receded into faraway voices, miniature faces on screens. Liam looked up, the sky so dense with stars it was hard to find the dark. A galaxy, a wonder of stars. A chill ran through Liam, ushering him back inside.

In the cold cabin, the shell of a person beckoned him, spectral in the moonlight. Drawn to it, Liam stepped closer, pressed his face up against the interior of the shell's mask, closed his eyes. The shell was made of everything. Plaster and wood and metal and stone and clay and cloth. He tried to smell his wife, but his nose was still steeped in bison. No matter how many times he inhaled—breathing in the smell of the mask and trying to force out the animal smell as he exhaled—the odor of the beasts lingered, obstinate and relentless.

Liam didn't remember lying down or falling back to sleep, but he awoke in the morning curled in the blanket on the cabin floor, the shell of a person looking down at him with empty eyes. He stood creakily, shook the memory of the bison away like airing out a rug, dust dissipating into dream. Liam cobbled together a breakfast of canned pears and jerky, then set about cleaning out the stove. It responded to his care like a neglected dog, offering its belly and happily stirring back to life. Liam filled it with wood from a well-seasoned stash he found behind the cabin, nursed the fire to crackling, and made coffee on the newly-cleaned surface. The remarkable ease with which the cabin welcomed him ignited in Liam the first inklings of joy he'd felt in many months. His meadow, his ghost town, were alive with morning birdsong and the sound of wind through conifers, an abundant calm.

As the sun climbed up over the ridge, Liam walked across the meadow to investigate what was left of the saloon. A scurry of chipmunks darted in and out of the ruin as Liam approached. Under the weight of years, the saloon had not fared well. Its tall façade still stood, but the double doors had mostly rotted away, and the sign was long gone, a rectangle of faded wood where it used to hang. All of the windows were broken or boarded up, and the whole building leaned to the side, pushed by weather and wind. Liam braved the brittle front porch and cautiously stepped inside.

You might expect such a building to be riddled with ghosts. A group of poltergeists is called a blanket. A group of phantoms is a rumpus. Spirits come in a penumbra. But those sorts of ghosts had all left long ago, taken back by the mountains and the warm sapphire sky. What Liam saw inside the saloon was just a scattering of physical things: tin cups, broken furniture, empty bottles. Shotgun shells. Bits of paper and cloth. Unidentifiable animal scat. Piles of tiny mouse bones, picked clean by ants.

Liam stepped behind the bar, surveyed the decaying room. In one corner, the remains of a piano, a rubble of strings and keys. His wife had loved listening to music while she worked. She had liked piano best, its capacity for both simple melodies and complex arrangements beneath the human hand. She would sculpt and weld and stitch for hours, the music pouring from her studio windows, sliding its way out from under her closed door to drift down the hall to the kitchen, where Liam would stand listening in the sun. A group of pianists is called a pound. The memory of the piano music felt heavy now, pressing on Liam's chest, the room spinning in sun-slivered light.

Liam's wife died three weeks after their son, following days of her struggling harder and harder to breathe. At first Liam thought it was the weight of her grief—so much time spent in bed, sobbing to the point of gasping. When she finally went to the hospital, there was nothing Liam or his daughter could do. They were not allowed to hug her, to hold her hands, to touch her at all, as she was taken away from them. They were not allowed to visit, to set foot within the hospital's walls. They tried to talk with her by video, but just a day after leaving them, Liam's wife was on a ventilator, unconscious.

Liam's heart imploded with the guilt of waiting too long, of not recognizing the hidden cause of her distress. When the call came that she had died—the doctor's voice a chisel driving at their crumbling family—Liam's daughter shut herself up in her room, afraid of every surface. Afraid of Liam, too. He sat in his wife's studio, himself afraid to touch the things she had touched, but also longing to hold every single thing.

Liam staggered from the saloon, anger and grief rising up in his throat. He tripped on the splintering floorboards and fell face-forward off the porch onto the ground. A group of grasses is called a fistful. A group of insects is a flight, a plague, a swarm. Liam grabbed at the grasses, yanked them out in clumps and threw them into the meadow. Swatted at the insects crawling on his sleeves. Yelled and yelled until his yelling was indistinguishable from its echo. A group of voices raised in song is called a harmony, a choir. But that isn't what this was.

*****

Liam's second night in the ghost town, he was visited by a pack of eerily light-haired wolves. The moon was perfectly full, brighter than the night before, and he was pulled from sleep by their howling. They howled together like any other wolves, though their voices were somehow hollow, transparent. It was as if they were whispering their howls, but the sound wasn't any less loud. A sound like the memory of a sound—something you can hear distinctly, even when it no longer fills your ears. The wolves sat together in the center of the meadow, and Liam watched them through the cabin's window. Their coats were yellowish-white, with blackish-buff hairs down their backs. They howled and howled for hours, a mournful keening. Liam cried quietly with them, grateful for someone to share in his sorrow as tears ran in slow rindles down his face. Then he dropped his head into his hands, and when he looked up again, the wolves were gone.

On the third night, Liam didn't even bother trying to sleep. He sat at the table with the three cremation boxes arrayed in front of him, staring at the initials until they hardly resembled letters anymore. The steadfast stove pulsed with firelight. Liam's bare feet were firm on the cabin's clean-swept floor. It was comforting to feel his feet against the cabin's base as it pressed its reliable foundation back at him. Beside the boxes Liam placed his son's ceramic bowl, his daughter's wooden box. Vessels. A group of vases is called a mingling, but only when broken. A group of bowls is called a nest. There is no distinct word for a group of boxes. We could call them a cradling. An embrace. Built to hold, to keep.

Liam's daughter had shared his knack for building things, his talent for joining one thing to the next in a perfection of pattern and design. The wooden box she'd built looked simple, but it was not. She'd assembled it without nails or screws, all dovetail joints rendered by hand. It was a thing of singular beauty.

Liam's daughter died a month after his wife, to the day. After his wife had passed, Liam and his daughter tried to stay in their separate rooms, worried they might contaminate each other. They tried to hold on to each other by not holding on to each other at all. But this was largely impossible. When his daughter started to cough, felt the pain swell in her chest, Liam couldn't stay away. He carried her to the car, drove her to the hospital before her symptoms were as bad as he knew they could become. Since she was only sixteen, he was allowed to stay at her bedside, which he did for two weeks. He covered his face with a mask, keeping all his fears tucked underneath. But she slipped away from him, too, in a room filled with doctors and nurses whose bodies were nearly invisible under all the protective gear. Doctors and nurses who couldn't save her, though Liam was broken with gratitude for how they tried.

At the cabin's table, Liam carefully lifted the lids of each cremation box. He stared down at the ashes, three individual piles which all looked more or less the same. The separateness of each box felt like a penance for his inability to keep his family whole. Gently,

Liam scooped the ashes into his palms and transferred them to the ceramic bowl his son had made, its gently sloping sides with their deep blue glaze receding like the sea as the pile of ashes grew. He mixed them together with his fingers, caressing each shard of carbon and bone. Liam folded the ashes into one another until they were a single mound, laid his hands on top of them, and closed his eyes. Tried to summon the voices, the bodies, of his wife and children. But they did not come.

There is no collective noun for ashes, nor for bones.

When Liam opened his eyes again, the window of the cabin was crowded with the muzzles of horses. With a dusting of ashes still on his hands, he opened the cabin door and stepped out into the night. Dozens of horses circled his cabin, their hides so glossy they reflected the stars. A herd of horses that were not ordinary horses. They were large, and robust, with lustrous brown necks resembling those of zebras, short manes bristling straight up toward the sky. The horses did not shy away as Liam reached for them. He ran his hands down their long noses, their strong necks, the ashes smearing across their star-dappled hides. He had nearly forgotten what it felt like to touch another being, to feel a quiver of life against his skin. But the horses were not alive. Even as he stroked them, their bodies retreated into nothingness. Liam's chest, his heart, swelled and then emptied as the faces of the horses faded, until all that was left were the stars.

Liam stepped back inside the cabin, his hands still curved to the shape of the horses' bodies, and returned to the ashes of everyone he loved most. He removed the lid of his daughter's wooden box. Then he lifted his son's ceramic bowl and tipped it so the joined ashes slid into the box. Replaced the lid to shelter them again. There's no proper name for this ritual, so we will have to make up our own. A mingling of ashes, the broken parts still calling to each other. A dovetailing of ashes. A slip of ashes, like the smoothing of clay before firing a vessel. A crossing. But there are other possibilities.

*****

At the far end of the meadow, which had once been the edge of the town, the mine opened its uneven mouth against the rocky slope. The morning after the horses, Liam's longing for his family pushed at the edges of his body, cresting in the chambers of his heart. There was only one place left in his ghost town that Liam hadn't yet looked for everyone he loved most. You might assume a cavern that had given up its gold but had taken many miners in return would be laden with ghosts. And at one point it had been, but those ghosts had made their peace with the mountain. Had laid their spirits back down atop their bones and allowed themselves to be reclaimed. So when Liam entered the mine, stood just inside its entrance and felt the cold wind of its breath, the only sadness he felt was his own.

Liam walked deeper into the mine, walked along the broken spine of cart tracks and rail spikes, until he was swathed by the dark. He reached out his hands to find the jagged rock of the tunnel wall and then sat down on the damp floor. Liam waited for his wife to come. He waited for his children. He was sure they would find him here in the darkness, would be drawn to the beacon of his pain. But a ghost is not the same as a moth. An eclipse of moths will throw their soft bodies against the lure of any light—an endless scorch of longing. But a ghost is different. A ghost can choose to take itself past that hungering, can choose to move through.

When Liam's wife was alive, she would turn to him in the night while they were sleeping, orient her body toward his body. Their children, when they were small, would cry out for him if they woke from discomfort or fear, and he'd gather them up in his arms. There is no name for a group of nightmares, nor of dreams. We could call them a reaching of nightmares. A compass of dreams.

Liam sat in the blackness until his whole body was numb and shivering, wracked with memory and grief. Nothing appeared to him. There was no one he could touch. Water dripped from the ceiling, and he listened to the dull splats of droplets hitting his boots, and to the echoing plinks of distant droplets falling farther inside the mine. If he followed the echoes, there might be a shaft, an unknown descent into the earth. Liam pictured himself plummeting, his body shattering the quiet of the mountain's core. His solitary body in the darkness, his cracked and lonely bones. But then he remembered the wooden box of ashes, safe and waiting for him on the cabin's enduring little table. He couldn't leave the ashes of his family moldering in a cabin in a ghost town, whittled at by marmots and mice. So Liam stood and felt his way back to the entrance of the mine, stepped again into the warm, gold light of the sun. He walked slowly across the meadow, keeping the cold absence at his back.

*****

Night after night, the ghosts of the animals came to Liam. Animals who had once lived in the meadow, or some iteration of the meadow, long, long ago. Animals who lived in the meadow before there was a mine, before there was a ghost town. Before there was Liam.

Some nights there were giant, ancient cats. A clowder. A pride. They startled Liam with their curving, saber teeth, their human-like cries. Other nights he witnessed rolls of beautiful armadillos, double the size of their nine-banded, extant relations.

Once a herd of Stegosaurs lumbered across the meadow, grazing on the grasses, towering over the slope of the cabin's roof. One passed right through the cabin itself, disturbing nothing, its massive body with its rows of scales remembering when the landscape was something else—a low plain crossed by slow-moving, muddy rivers. Some nights there were ground sloths. There is no collective noun for ground sloths, but we could invent one. A reluctance of ground sloths. A linger. A gradation. The sloths made their way across the meadow slowly, their pace echoing the reknitting of Liam's heart.

Finally came the night of the largest group of ghosts: the yellowfin cutthroat trout. A hover of trout. It was late autumn, the skies tipping toward winter. Snow had begun to fall. The bodies of the fish glistened amber, speckled with dark beads—the reverse of a sky filled with stars. The shoal of fish swam through the cold mountain night, weaving in and out of snowflakes, their tails whipping the air. An avalanche of snowflakes. A drift of fish. Liam stood among them, felt their shining bodies flex against his face as they moved past. Watched as they schooled in and out of his visible, living breath. The fish were small enough to fit within Liam's hands, but they twisted smoothly out of his grasp.

Before his children, before his wife, when Liam was very young, his parents often brought him into these mountains to hike. Down trails quilted with fragrant needles of spruce and pine.

Through rocky passes above the timberline brimming with wildflowers and pocked by the tawny, darting backsides of pika. Once to a glacial lake teeming with trout. In a little wooden rowboat, its bench seats painted the same soft blue as the sky, Liam caught his very first fish. Its body thrashed and pulled at the end of his line. He remembered the cold, slippery weight of it in his hands. The stilling of its dappled fins, its mouth opening and closing in gulps and pauses as he held it. Held on to it while it died, his own mouth falling open in anguish and awe.

The night after the trout, there were no ghosts, though Liam waited for them, standing at the cabin window watching the snow. The last of the aspen leaves unlatched themselves into the frigid air, settled on the meadow's frosty ground. Another thing you should understand about ghosts is that they know when to leave. Liam listened to his heart beat and beat, an unfailing metronome, a lonely measuring of time until dawn.

When morning came at last, Liam walked to the center of the meadow, his daughter's wooden box in his arms. The wind was building, rushing down from the peaks. Liam opened the box, offered the ashes to the air. They swirled up, twined with the flurries of snow. Liam watched as they whirled and lifted. He watched until all of the ashes had scattered through the ghost town, through the tired planks of the saloon, into the mouth of the mine, up over the trees. Watched until his body felt peaceful and calm. Then he carried the empty box back into the cabin.

Liam set his daughter's box on the table next to his son's bowl. Beside the table stood the shell of a person his wife had made. He stepped inside, kissed the inverse of its lips. Stepped out again. He secured the cabin and walked out into the snow, pried open the door of his truck.

The roads were not yet icy, but still Liam drove slowly. Everyone he loved most had died, but Liam felt something gathering within him, keeping company with his heart. When he reached the city, the streets were quiet. A person here, a person there. Half-hidden faces wherever he turned his reddened eyes. So Liam had to imagine clusters of children playing. Had to summon the figures of adults bunched together again, arms around one another in the cold but sunny afternoon.

A group of people can be many things: a crowd, a company, a band, a tribe. A body. Perhaps Liam drove until he found a house he remembered. Perhaps he parked his truck, knocked on the patient door. Perhaps when the door opened, you shouted his name: *Liam!* Perhaps he stepped into your arms.

But there are other possibilities.

The Last

When the northern white rhino shows up, Fin is ready for the rites. The animal's massive horn materializes first, followed by small, black eyes and then heavy, three-toed hooves. Fin had been watching the free-standing archway, waiting for the beast to step through the gnarled wooden aperture into the plain of light. Now, she stands before the arch, holding a tall stone pitcher of water. The gray armor of the rhino's shoulders emerges, then thick, wrinkled flanks, a curl of tail. The rhino is nervous, confused, its eyes wide and wary. But Fin is never afraid of what comes through the arch. She steps toward the rhino, carrying the stone vessel with practiced ease.

Fin can't remember ever being anywhere but here. She has always been the receiver, the celebrant, the caretaker of the beings that come through the arch. Fin is a fulcrum, standing in the middle of the plain of light, the horizon gleaming beyond the arch. And beyond that horizon, the creatures she's already ushered through call to her, lonely in each other's company as they wait for her to return. Their voices tug at her, and she aches to go to them. A few decades back she could spend whole days among them, smoothing their feathers and stroking their fur. But new animals come through so often now that Fin can never leave the arch, can scarcely keep up with the rites.

The rhino takes a tentative step forward, lowers its head before Fin. She places a hand on its front horn, then tilts the pitcher over the rhino's forehead and pours slowly, so the water rivers between its ears and down its face. Fin walks along the length of the great ungulate, pouring water over its back down to its tail, which relaxes as the last of the liquid drips down its leathery skin. The rhino shivers its hide, and its body begins to shimmer. The animal lifts its head toward the sounds coming from beyond the plain's edge. It looks back for a moment at Fin, who stands quietly, holding the empty pitcher. Then the rhino takes off in a run, charging across the plain of light.

The sorrow that inhabits Fin whenever an animal comes through the arch sometimes feels too heavy to hold. She remembers them all: the Pyrenean ibex with knobby, ringed horns who's back sagged with the ghost-weight of the fallen tree that killed it; the

Tasmanian tiger still stinking of zoo as Fin washed its banded fur; the Xerces blue butterfly that landed on Fin's shoulder, allowed the anointing of its delicate wings. And many centuries before, the flightless dodo, stumbling through the archway, unafraid. All of them burdened with their solitary passings. All of them the last of their kind.

Fin walks a few paces to where a bright turquoise pool glistens on the plain of light. She dips her pitcher, fills it once again to the brim. For some time now, at least three creatures have come through the arch every hour. Insects with colorful bodies, birds with astonishing feathers or feathers muted as stone, frogs no bigger than Fin's thumbnail. Creatures from the oceans' depths, floating through the arch in search of the sea. Fin tends to all of them, sends them off across the plain of light.

*****

Fin fills pitcher after pitcher of water as the pace of creatures entering the plain of light quickens. Sometimes animals from different continents come through the archway together, tangling with confusion and alarm. Fin cannot properly receive them; cannot give them the attention they deserve. She is coaxing a hawksbill turtle from the muscular arms of a mountain gorilla when a bird flies through the arch and continues right over Fin's head, toward the clamorous horizon. Fin cannot tell what species of bird it was, may never find it again. She worries what will happen when it crests the horizon, unanointed. Fin's pitcher is empty again. She lifts it with faltering hands.

A cheetah arrives at full sprint, streaking past her in a blur that becomes the plain of light itself. Fin rushes to refill the pitcher, but the turquoise pool is empty. Fin stands rooted, wrestling with the unfamiliar disquiet that rises through her. The air is crowded with insect noise, squawking, and howls. Her head rings with the sounds of bats and dolphins trying to echolocate across the plain of light. Fin can feel the many species of whales calling to one another beyond the horizon, each in their own beautiful language. Then the plain shudders. Fin loses her balance, falls to the ground beside the arch.

A cascade of creatures streams through the opening, a mass of feathers and fur and scales. There are so many of them, the ground disappears. The sky becomes a riot of wings. Fin struggles to her feet just as an elephant lumbers through the arch, swinging its trunk sadly from side to side, regarding her with vast, liquid eyes. Fin runs her hands along its flanks, but it shies away from her, turns its head toward the horizon. No animal has ever refused Fin's comfort, her touch. She reaches for the pitcher, but it lies shattered at her feet.

And for the first time in her existence on the plain of light, Fin is afraid.

For many moments, nothing else comes through the arch. All the creatures approach from beyond the horizon and fall silent, watching Fin. She turns her attention again to the archway, for now something else is approaching. Fin steps toward the arch to meet it, and relief washes over her like water. The creature before her is upright, skin smooth and barren except for long hairs sprouting from the slope of its skull. Its eyes are terrified, remorseful, and it hesitates before the creatures on the plain of light. As it passes through the arch, it flounders, and Fin reaches out. She takes its trembling fingers within her empty hands.

Acknowledgments

With thanks to the following publications for giving some of these stories their first homes:

About Place Journal: "Suffer"

Chautauqua: "Over and Back"

The Dodge: "The Vault"

If the Storm Clears (Blue Cactus Press): "The Torture Orchard"

Kestrel: "Animal Rain"

Permafrost: "Woolly"

Santa Monica Review: "Flight Path"

Sinking City: "The Last"

Terrain.org: "The Ghost Town Collectives"

Special Thanks

Immense gratitude to the past and present members of my writing critique group, the Guttery. These stories would never have come to fruition without the insightful comments and guidance of Tola Molotkov, Michael Keefe, Cheyenne Montgomery, Jessie Glenn,

Shari MacDonald Strong, Jennifer Brennock, Tammy Lynne Stoner, Jackleen de la Harpe, Lauren Fulton, and Sherri Hoffman.

Thanks to Margaret Malone, who first unfolded the roadmap to these stories in her exceptional fiction craft workshops. Participants in those workshops helped with early versions of two of these stories at the very genesis of this collection.

Many thanks to editor David Martin for loving this collection and bringing me into the Middle Creek Publishing fold.

I'm bottom-of-my-heart grateful to PLAYA and Mineral School for the residencies that afforded me time to work on these stories in the company of inspiring writers and artists.

To my high school English teacher father, thank you for introducing me to short stories when I was very young and kindling my love for the genre. And to my mother, thank you for digging that crumpled up story of mine out of the garbage can years ago, believing in me as a writer before I did.

To my family, Thomas, Elliot, and Onyx, thank you for your support and encouragement, especially through the years of the pandemic, as I holed up to research and write.

To David, for listening as I read each story aloud, thank you for your curiosity, your attentiveness, and for touching me back.

And praise to every landscape, real and imaginary, that served as muse for these stories, especially the places to which I've not yet traveled. I'm ready for my field trip now.

About the Author

Brittney Corrigan is the author of the poetry collections *Daughters*, *Breaking*, *Navigation*, *40 Weeks* and most recently, *Solastalgia*, a collection of poems about climate change, extinction, and the Anthropocene Age (JackLeg Press, 2023). Brittney was raised in Colorado and has lived in Portland, Oregon for the past three decades, where she is an alumna and employee of Reed College. *The Ghost Town Collectives* is her first short story collection.

For more information, visit: www.brittneycorrigan.com

About the Press

Middle Creek Publishing believes that responding to the world through art & literature—and sharing that response—is a vital part of being an artist.

Middle Creek Publishing is a company seeking to make the world a better place through both the means and ends of publishing. We are publishers of quality literature in any genre from authors and artists, both seasoned and those who are undiscovered or under-valued, or under-represented, with a great interest in works which illuminate or embody any aspect of contemplative Human Ecology, defined as the relationship between humans and their natural, social, and built environments.

Middle Creek Publishing's particular interest in Human Ecology is meant to clarify an aspect of the quality in the works we will consider for publication and as a guide to those considering submitting work to us. Our interest is in publishing works which illuminate the human experience through words, story or other content that connects us to each other, our environment, our history, and our potential deeply and more consciously.

www.ingramcontent.com/pod-product-compliance
Lightning Source LLC
Chambersburg PA
CBHW050339030726
47503CB00008B/2529